Wordeater

© 2018 by H. Duke

Cover image © 2018 by H. Duke

ISBN-13: 978-1-947094-20-8

Hdukeauthor.com

WordEater
Book Three in the Library Gate Series
H. Duke

Table of Contents

Dear reader

Thank you for reading *Wordeater,* the third book in the Library Gate Series. You can sign up for my reader group at www.hdukeauthor.com. I regularly host giveaways and send out free stories.

When you're done reading, I'd appreciate if you'd leave an honest review, because it helps other readers find a book they'll like.

Enjoy the story!

-H. Duke

Chapter One

"Must you go, sorceress?" the genie asked. He ran his fingers over her bare collarbone, making her shiver.

April checked her watch. "I wish I could stay. I have to get back." She grimaced.

"You seem unhappy about it."

She shrugged. "It's Dorian. It's like he's judging me whenever I walk back into the library."

She stood and reached for her clothes, but the genie grabbed her wrists and pulled her back down. "We could make him come search for you again. I'd love to see the jealous look on his face."

"No, I really need to get back, and—wait, what do you mean jealous look? Jealous of what?"

"Is it not obvious?" The genie raised his eyebrows suggestively.

"Is what not obvious?"

"He's infatuated with you."

Her cheeks got hot. "What? No way. Why would you say that?" She pulled her clothes on more quickly than she'd planned to.

"I saw it from the moment I first laid eyes on the boy. I thought you knew. It's hard to miss."

"He's hardly a boy," April said.

"Compared to me he is." the genie stretched.

"Big-headed much?"

The genie laughed. "My head is not the only thing about me that's big."

April groaned. "For someone who's bragging about his manliness, you certainly have the humor of a fifteen-year-old boy."

"Don't be sore, Sorceress. I thought you knew about his fixation. It's truly unmistakable."

"Well, you're wrong."

"If you say so," the genie shrugged. "Shall I take you back to your little doorway?"

"No. I'll walk." He couldn't be right about Dorian, could he?

She barely noticed the dusty Ottoman city bustling around her as she made her way back to the gate. The genie was just trying to get under her skin, but she couldn't get his words out of her head.

If she was honest with herself, there had been moments of tension between her and Dorian. She'd assumed it was because of the ink rot, or whatever stressful situations they'd been dealing with at the time.

And why did she care so much, anyway? Why did she dread Dorian's disapproval? She wasn't the type to let others shame her for the choices she made.

It's because you don't want things to be strained between you and Dorian, she told herself. Yeah, that was it. Made total sense.

Still, she hesitated when she arrived at the gate. But she couldn't stay in the world of *One Thousand and One Nights* forever. With a sigh, she stepped through the veil.

Dorian sat at one of the tables, a stack of books in front of him. He looked up at her through his reading glasses.

"Hey," she said, her face getting hot.

"Did you have a pleasant time?"

She nodded, her cheeks hot.

He looked back down at the book in front of him. "Good. See you tomorrow evening."

"See you tomorrow."

She gathered up her things. There was no way the genie was right. Was there? There was something in the way Dorian had looked away from her... but she must have imagined it.

Chapter Two

"*Another* book?"

April placed a finger in the book in question—*Frankenstein* by Mary Shelley—and glanced across the kitchen table at Gram. Gram frowned as she poured herself a second mug of green tea. "I don't want to seem unsupportive of reading, but it's all you do lately. That, and visit your *boyfriend*."

April winced at the boyfriend comment—especially after the previous evening's conversation with the genie—but she could relate to Gram's annoyance at her constant reading. She'd thought Dorian was joking about assigning her a reading list. He wasn't.

Out loud she said, "It's for work. They want each library staff member to be knowledgeable about at least one area of literature. Lucky me, I drew the classics." She sighed. She was sure Janet, Becky, and everyone else who worked at the library knew more about just about any genre than she did, including the classics.

"Well, you'd think that since they made it a requirement, they'd give you time at work to read. You know, when you're getting *paid*."

"Gram, when I started this job I knew I'd have to read more. I'm a librarian now, for crying out loud." She grimaced at hearing the phrase she hated so much coming out of her own mouth.

Gram sighed. "I know. It's just I never see you anymore, and when I do, you've got your nose in some book."

Now that the ink rot was under control, April no longer stayed at the library into the wee hours of the morning, but she rarely came home before midnight. Even though she tried to force herself out of bed by nine, it wasn't always possible. Oftentimes she'd sleep through her alarm and have barely enough time to eat lunch before heading to work.

"Sorry, Gram," she said. "I'll wake up earlier. I promise."

"I know you're up late visiting your *friend*," Gram said, emphasizing the word. "But do you have to see him every night? I miss you. And..."

Gram trailed off, but April knew what she was thinking. She didn't have a lot of time left. It was easy to forget Gram's prognosis of a few months at best (and one month was already gone... time was moving too fast) because she looked so healthy. But the doctors had assured them that the cancer still lurked inside, growing stronger each day. It was biding its time, and one day it would attack, like some James Bond villain. The doctors said they were lucky Gram felt as good as she did.

Yeah. *Lucky*.

Guilt and something darker and more depressing flooded April's stomach. "Sorry, Gram. I'll cut it back."

"You must really like him," Gram mused, prying clandestinely.

"Yeah," April said evasively. She still didn't know the genie's name, and she wanted to keep it that way. The last thing she needed was more complication in her life. That's why she liked his company: it was uncomplicated.

"I'm looking forward to finally meeting him tomorrow." Gram stressed the word *finally*.

Barty had agreed to pose as April's boyfriend. Ostensibly it was so he could place a protective enchantment over the house—April had taken Thaddeus' warning about the collectors targeting Gram to heart—but it also had the side benefit of fulfilling Gram's desire to meet her significant other. April just wanted to get the whole evening over with. She still hadn't thought of a way to tell Barty he'd be going by "Dorian" for the night. She winced at the memory of blurting out Dorian's name the night Gram had grilled her about her new "boyfriend."

It was bad enough on its own, but after the conversation with the genie...

From the living room, they heard the metallic clank of the mailbox outside the front door. Gram went to get the mail and April sighed and went over her schedule quickly in her head. "Why don't we go to the mall sometime this week? How about Wednesday?" she said when Gram walked back into the kitchen.

Gram stopped rifling through the mail and raised her eyebrow. "Are you sure we can afford a shopping trip?"

April shrugged. "We can't go crazy, obviously, but we can afford to window shop... and maybe treat ourselves to lunch in the food court. What do you say? It will be like when I was a little kid."

Gram smiled. "Okay, hon. It's a date." She walked over to the calendar on the fridge and wrote *mall with April* in thick permanent marker.

~~~

April looked up from *Frankenstein*. She'd gotten so caught up in the downfall of Victor Frankenstein that she'd lost track of what was happening in the Werner Room. From her vantage point at the reference desk, she could see that the tables and arm chairs were nearly empty. Randall sat in his usual spot in the nearest armchair, and Rex was next to him, snout resting peacefully on his paws. Randall flipped through a magazine he'd brought up from the second floor.

April returned to *Frankenstein,* surprised by how drawn into the book she'd become. In fact, most of the books she'd read weren't as boring as she'd expected. In the last week she'd finished *The Time Machine, The War of the Worlds,* and several works by Edgar Allen Poe. Most started slow, but once she got into them they weren't too bad.

She jumped when Becky's voice came over the walkie talkie sitting in its dock station. "Fifteen minutes to close."

April placed an index card in *Frankenstein*, ready to start her closing checklist. To her surprise, Becky addressed her directly.

"Hey, April—is Randall up there?"

April grabbed the walkie talkie. "Yeah. Why?"

"Can you send him down? There are a few rowdy teenagers and I'd feel better if he were here when I give them the boot."

Ever since Randall had stopped Rico's mother from attacking April, Becky had been requesting Randall's presence whenever she was in a situation that might escalate. A few of the other nighttime L.A.s had started to do the same.

"Sure, I'll ask him. It's empty up here." She put the walkie talkie back on its charging stand and called over to Randall. "Do you mind going down to the first floor? There are some teens Becky thinks might give her trouble."

Randall puffed up slightly. "Sure," he said, and he and Rex made their way to the stairwell.

April smiled as he went, and then started on the closing check list.

~~~

They'd dealt with the night's allotment of ink rot in less than a half hour and now she, Barty, Dorian, Randall, and Rex sat around the coffee table in the reading nook. Dorian had a complex system for deciding how much rot to take care of on any given night.

As far as she could tell, his system involved a rotating schedule of checking books. He'd go through them one by one and examine them for the black, ink splotch-like stains that indicated the rot had taken hold. Infected books were categorized by degree of severity, which was how he decided which ones needed immediate attention and which ones could be put off until later. For all she knew, he started with the A's and when he got to the Zs, started all over again from the beginning.

"Let's go over the plan for tomorrow night once more," Dorian said. "Just to be sure we're all on the same page."

April nodded. "Barty's going to come over for dinner. I'll give him a tour of the house. He can place the spell then."

Barty spoke up. His ears were a vibrant shade of red. "I still think it's a better idea for me to cast the spell while delivering a pizza. I mean, what if your grandmother recognizes me from a delivery anyway?"

April snorted. "Gram's never ordered a pizza in her entire life. Calls it a heart attack in a box. Anyway, you need to enter every room in the house, right?"

Barty nodded. "Closets, pantries, basements—you get the idea. Anything with a door that's large enough for an adult to step through."

"Well, it would be strange if I invited the pizza delivery guy in to see my closet, don't you think?"

Barty nodded, though he didn't look happy about it.

Randall rubbed his chin. "Can you explain again why you can't do the same protection spell you placed on the library on their house?"

Barty shook his head. "That spell requires several magical components that I no longer possess, thanks to the collectors. It would be nearly impossible for me to find replacements. Definitely not before tomorrow night. Believe me, I've been trying."

Randall ran his fingers through his hair. "So what *will* this enchantment do?"

Barty pulled out the volume of his grandfather's grimoire from his satchel and opened it. He held up the book for them to see: *Spell of Warning,* it said.

"This is similar to the charm I put on April's amulet, except it's more powerful and more complex. It's location-specific rather than person-specific. It takes a lot more power and preparation, though. If I set it up correctly, it will warn April if the collectors get anywhere near her house." He stood. "That said, I still have some preparations to do—plus a good night's sleep wouldn't be a bad thing. I think we should call it a night, unless there's something else to discuss."

April shook her head. "I don't have anything else."

Dorian nodded. "Me neither."

Barty was Randall's ride, so they left together. After they walked out, April and Dorian were alone in the Werner Room.

"Do you need any help?" April asked, avoiding his eyes.

He shook his head. "There's not much to find. We really pared down the rot."

"Okay, then." She stood and hesitated. She wanted to ask him about what the genie said, but knew it wasn't a good idea. If the answer was yes—that he did have feelings for her—what good would it do to bring it up? And if the answer was no, it would just make things awkward between them...

Before she could make up her mind about asking, Dorian spoke. "Are you visiting the genie tonight?" The words were casual, like he was asking her if she was stopping to get gas on the way home. Like he didn't care either way. Did that mean the genie was wrong? Or was it *too* casual, calculated?

She shook her head. "I told Gram I'd get up earlier to spend more time with her. The genie will understand."

"Oh."

"Well, good night." She started to walk away but then turned back around. The words tumbled from her mouth before she could stop them. "Why do you care if I go see the genie or not?"

Dorian looked up at her through his reading glasses. "I don't. I just want to know if I'll have access to my study."

"Oh." Of course that's what it was. Why had she let the genie's words get to her? Heat rose in her cheeks. Thank God she hadn't actually asked if he liked her or something!

Dorian frowned at her, his eyes magnified slightly through his glasses. "Why? Is something bothering you?"

She shook her head. "No. I mean... I was just wondering. I'd better get home. Good night."

He looked back down at the book in front of him. "Good night, Ms. Walker."

Chapter Three

Thaddeus stood outside of the warehouse. The large, non-descript building was where the agency stored the magical items deemed suitable for mission use. He knew keeping magic around was a necessity, but he was glad he'd never had cause to go beyond the front office where the pleasant receptionists checked out the items he needed. Even being here, just knowing what was inside, was uncomfortable, like standing next to a live bomb.

Mason was late. He always was whenever he set up appointments somewhere other than his own office. In a way it was good, because he seemed to think that the lateness was enough posturing and didn't lecture Thaddeus about random bullshit.

Finally, a car pulled up. It was a Benz, one of Mason's less ostentatious cars. He imagined Mason going on and on to his poor assistant that a Ferrari or Porsche would look out of place in the warehouse district and wrinkled his nose.

"Thad!" Mason exclaimed when he stepped out of the car. "Good to see you, son! Thanks for meeting me here."

He ushered Thaddeus through the front door. The interior resembled the lobby of an auto repair shop. Other than a vending machine, water cooler, and coffee maker, the room was fairly spartan. Nothing in the sad-looking chairs hinted at what lay behind the office doors.

Thaddeus recognized the woman behind the safety glass over the desk. Her name was Whitney, or maybe Wendy. Something that started with a W. He nodded to her.

"Good evening, Mr. Broker." She smiled at him politely, then directed her attention to Mason. "What can we do for you today, Mr. Mason?"

Thaddeus expected him to ask her to fetch something from the back, some obscure magical item that would be helpful in acquiring the library portal. As though he knew enough about working in the field to make such decisions.

Instead, he said, "We'd like the tour today, Whitney."

Tour? Why would Mason take him into the warehouse? Field agents, even those as high up as Thaddeus was, didn't have access. Thaddeus' skin crawled at the thought.

"Of course." Whitney smiled at Mason, then glanced at Thaddeus with more appreciation. "I'll grab someone. Please help yourselves to the snack bar."

Neither of them touched the snack bar. Mason kept playing around with his phone, telling Thaddeus that his daughter was having some trouble at school. Thaddeus was happy enough to stare off into space and wonder why Mason was letting him into the back. What could he possibly have to show him back there?

Maybe he was going to explain to him the necessity of keeping a few items around, how important it was in giving them an edge against the people they were up against. He didn't need to bother; Thaddeus had long since accepted that it was the only way to even the playing field. It was his burden to bear to be one of the few people who were truly against magic who had to sometimes wield it. It was an irony of nature, a price he had to pay.

Finally, a woman he hadn't seen before came out through the only door behind the desk. Her nametag read "Jane." She was dressed business-casual in khaki pants, a white polo, and sensible, sturdy shoes. She smiled politely at them; apparently fawning over them like Whitney did was not in her job description.

"Follow me," she said, opening the waist-high swinging door that led behind the bullet-proof glass. Thaddeus did as he was told. Why did he feel like he'd just stepped over some kind of line?

The woman gestured to a second door in the wall behind the desk. Thaddeus blinked. There had been only one door there only moments ago. Or had there? He thought back to all the times he'd visited the warehouse on mission business. He was sure there had been only one.

He glanced at Mason, who grinned back at him, waiting for a reaction. Thaddeus merely smiled. If Mason wanted a show of surprise, he'd come to the wrong person.

Jane held the door open as they walked through it and into a long, thin hallway. The hallway was lit with long strips of fluorescent lights, painted cinder-block walls, and polished concrete floors. Every so often they passed a door, but for the most part the hallway was just that, a hallway.

After several minutes of walking, they came to a second doorway made of heavy metal, painted a rusty shade of orange.

Jane turned to Mason. "Would you like to do the honors, sir?"

"You go ahead, sweetheart," Mason said with a patronizing smile.

She pulled out an oversized keyring, the kind that a janitor might carry, jingling with hundreds of keys of all shapes and sizes, including what looked like hotel room card keys. While some were ornate, the majority were simple house keys.

Jane singled out one of the card keys. She held it up in front of a card reader against the wall next to the door. The doors slid open to reveal that the hallway continued on the other side. They started walking again.

This stretch of hallway looked the same as the first, except that the floor sloped downwards. Thaddeus thought of the second door behind the reception desk. He bet that it led to a fake warehouse. What would it contain? Wood? Exotic imports? Car parts? Something that would look like it belonged in the warehouse district in case someone got curious and stopped by to check on things.

They came to a wall—a dead end. Thaddeus glanced at Jane and Mason. Neither of them acted perturbed by this. Well, if they weren't going to bring it up he sure as hell wasn't.

Jane pulled out the keyring again. This time she unclipped a long, thin key that resembled a stylus. She took it and carefully spelled something out on the wall—her name? A password? The stylus did not leave any marks, so it was impossible to know for sure—on the wall.

She pulled the key away with a flourish, and the wall dissolved, revealing an elevator on the other side. They stepped inside. The walls were completely smooth—no buttons, not even an emergency phone. What would happen if they got stuck?

The elevator door slid closed, and he fought the urge to throw himself back out into the hallway and run for the exit. The hair on his arms stood on end—he could practically feel the magic swirling in the air around him.

"Going down," Mason said, then laughed as though it were the funniest joke in the world. Jane chuckled politely.

At first, his stomach dropped like they were moving downwards, but then it felt like they weren't moving at all. It was like being on one of those amusement park rides where they put you in a room and shake you around a little to simulate movement.

"How far down does this go?" Thaddeus asked.

Jane smiled. "It depends what you're looking for."

What kind of answer was that? She offered no other clarification. "What's above us?" he asked. "Just dirt?"

She laughed uncomfortably. "Perhaps you should ask Mr. Mason these questions. He'll be able to answer them more to your satisfaction."

Or, more likely, she wouldn't have to tread so carefully about how much information to give him.

Mason spoke up. "All in good time, Thad. Be patient. Don't ruin the surprise!"

Mason wanted him to ask what the surprise was, like a five-year-old, didn't he? Thaddeus didn't say anything.

Finally, Jane took out the stylus-like key and wrote something on the elevator door. When she pulled away, the wall began to dissolve, revealing a large warehouse space. If it weren't for the lack of windows and the fact that Thaddeus knew better, he would have assumed that they were on the ground level.

There was one issue with that, though: this space was far larger than the warehouse above was.

They stepped out of the elevator onto a platform that overlooked the warehouse floor.

It was so much larger than he could have imagined. Rows of gigantic shelves stacked with boxes and crates towered at least three stories high. Each row continued on further than he could see. A dozen workers wearing yellow hard hats and lab coats moved about the floor.

Jane stepped around a corner and came back with two hard hats and two pairs of protective eye goggles. She wore an identical set. "Safety first," she said cheerfully.

Mason took one set and handed the other to Thaddeus.

"Thanks for your help, Jane. Now, I need to discuss a few things with Thad in private. We'll find you again when we need to be let out."

She nodded and walked away, her footsteps echoing in the massive space.

"What is this place?" Thaddeus asked.

"It's the warehouse where we store our magical acquisitions."

"I know that. But all this can't all be filled with magic. It's too big. What is the rest of the space used for?"

"Walk with me, Thad." Mason led Thaddeus down a flight of industrial metal stairs onto the warehouse's main floor. He could see the activity of the floor below through the mesh steel steps.

Workers holding clipboards walked by them. They appeared to be counting or otherwise recording the boxes' conditions. Most wore lab coats, hard hats, and eye visors. Did they know those items were useless to protect them against the evils that lined the shelves?

Damn it. Twenty minutes ago he had no idea that this place existed. His ears buzzed as he became light-head, still unable to believe what he was seeing.

A horn beeped behind them, and Thaddeus moved to let a forklift pass. The vehicle stopped about twenty feet away, raising the forklift up and pulling a large metal box from one of the higher shelves.

"What's he doing?" Thaddeus asked. Why would they need to move one of these objects?

"Perhaps someone in another division needs it for a mission," Mason said. "Who knows? You're always so *focused* on the details, Thad! That's why I brought you here today."

"It is?" Thad watched the forklift recede into the distance.

He walked to the base of the shelving. A clipboard hanging on a hook read *statues—cursed, enchanted, otherwise spelled*. Thaddeus started to ask what use a cursed statue could serve to another division, but he stopped himself. It was against protocol to ask about another operative's work. It could endanger the mission.

Instead, he said, "Why haven't these items been destroyed? They're dangerous."

Mason shrugged and looked over at Thad. "You've had as much experience with magic as me, possibly more."

Definitely more, Thaddeus thought, but he didn't dare say it out loud.

Mason continued. "Have you ever seen a magical object decommissioned?"

"That's not my department," Thaddeus said. "I acquire the objects and then deliver them. After that they're someone else's problem."

"You're a good soldier, Thad," Mason said, clapping him on the back. "You do what you're told and believe everything, or at least don't ask questions. That sort of numb obedience is important at a certain level, don't get me wrong. But I'm going to pull back the curtain a bit."

Thaddeus was stunned. A soldier? Numb obedience?

Mason continued. "Magic, in its very basic form, is energy. Energy cannot be destroyed."

"But it can be converted," Thaddeus said.

"True," Mason said, "But what's conversion of magic other than wizardry? And who knows, we might accidentally convert these things into something even more unstable. It's best to keep them here, where they're safe."

Thaddeus took a step towards Mason. "So you're telling me that none of the items I've turned in have been destroyed? They're all just sitting here in this warehouse?"

One of the nearby workers glanced at them nervously before tucking his clipboard under his arm and striding away. Thaddeus realized he'd raised his voice.

"Whoah, sport." He patted Thaddeus on the shoulder again. "It must come as a shock... but part of you must have known deep down. You're too smart."

Thaddeus thought of all the times the opposition had accused him of stealing their magic. Collectors, they called them. He always hated the name, but took solace in the fact that it was a misnomer. Why let the words of filthy magic wielders get to him?

But they were right.

Mason was still talking. "It's here so we can protect it."

"You mean protect the world from it," Thaddeus corrected.

"Of course." Mason waved his hand dismissively as though there was barely a distinction.

"What if someone finds this?" Thaddeus asked. "What if someone breaks in? What if one of the workers becomes power-hungry—"

"Calm down. None of that is going to happen. Did you see all the hullabaloo Jane went through just to get us down here? And that's with *knowing* what needs to be done. And the workers are paid very, very well. But if they do get ideas... well, let's just say they won't like the results."

Was Mason implying that the workers would be harmed if they tried to steal any of the items? No, that wasn't possible. The agency protected people; it didn't hurt them.

Thaddeus gritted his teeth. "Why are you telling me this?"

"I think I've made you wait long enough for your surprise," Mason said, gleefully, ignoring his question "Do you have any guesses? No?"

Why didn't Mason just get on with it, already?

Mason looped an arm around Thaddeus' neck, then steered him away from the shelf. "You've been one of our most effective operatives. You've deserved a promotion ten times over, but we've kept you in the field because you're so damn effective. You make me look good to the partners. But it's time you reap some of the benefits of your hard work and dedication." He spread his arms wide. "Say hello to your new office!"

Thaddeus stopped. "You're taking me out of the field? Sir—"

"We're promoting you, son."

"But the Pagewalker—"

"You'll be more effective against her this way. Don't think I didn't take that into account. We've already assigned a new lead to your squadron."

"But—"

"I'm promoting you, Thad. Try to show a little bit of gratitude." There was a note of warning in Mason's voice. This wasn't an offer.

Thaddeus swallowed. "What exactly does this promotion entail?"

"You'll be undertaking a more... managerial role," Mason said. "We'll go over it in more detail later, but in a nutshell, you'll put your experience to better use overseeing magical acquisitions and storage."

Mason's meaning started to sink in. "You mean you want me to work here? Surrounded by all this?" Thaddeus said. He glanced up at the shelves. They now seemed to be pressing in on him, threatening to fall down and crush him.

"No. You'll have your own office in a separate part of the building. Like I said, all those details still need to be worked out. I just thought you needed perspective on the true scope of your job to understand what an honor this is. We're not just pushing you off to some desk."

Thaddeus' heart sank. Even if he wasn't working here with all this evil surrounding him, this meant no more field work. How was he supposed to fulfill his father's legacy from behind a stack of papers?

"Your yearly salary will double," Mason said, his voice raising in pitch enticingly.

Thaddeus forced himself to nod. There was no use arguing with Mason now. All he could do was let him play out his show and hope he could fix this later when Mason was in a less dramatic mood. "Thank you, sir."

Mason clapped him on the back once more. "That's more like it. Now, I hate to run off, but the headmistress at my daughter's school has a vendetta against her," he explained with a grim look on his face. "the bitch says she's been bullying the other girls. She's suspended her for a week. Can you believe it? I have to fly there and straighten this out. I swear they do this so they can extort money out of me." He sighed. "My assistant will be in touch to schedule a follow-up appointment."

Mason waved his hand. "Have a look around. When you're done, just let Jane know you want to leave. You don't want to get stuck in the elevator."

Thaddeus stared after him as he left, dumb-struck. Once Mason disappeared, he glanced around the shelves. He wanted to leave, but... he felt he needed to get a handle on just how big this place was.

He started down the aisle. He walked for nearly twenty minutes and still he could see no end to the shelves stacked with boxes. Was that magic too? How much more was there? And this couldn't be the only such facility like this, could it? Europe would have one, as well as the other major city centers in the states. So much magic concentrated in one spot. Centuries' worth. He'd thought he'd been working to destroy it. What a joke.

They'd called them the collectors. They were right.

He walked to the nearest clipboard. *Moles, curse breakers, and counter-spells.* Those were at least useful, he supposed. But what about the rest of it?

He continued walking until he came to a break in the shelves. He turned left, moving towards what he thought was the center. The next several rows he passed were the same as the first, stacks upon stacks of boxes, barrels, and crates.

But then the rows opened onto a square structure, a building within a building. It could have been a direct-access motel where the rooms opened to the parking lot. It stood three stories, each holding around twenty doors. A fetid human odor permeated the air, the smell of body odor and excrement.

In the center of each door was a small window with bars, below which was a small, thin slot. A worker pushed a cart around the first level. At each door he removed a tray from the slot, then pressed a new one in. What was he doing?

A second worker climbed up the stairs to the second level, his feet clanging on the mesh metal stairs with every step. A keyring identical to Jane's dangled from his belt. How many such keyrings existed? What security measures were in place to make sure that one didn't end up in the wrong hands?

The worker stopped in front of one of the doors, checked his clipboard, then unlocked the door. He pulled out an old man, roughly pushing him up against the wall. The prisoner was so thin that Thaddeus feared he might snap in half from the rough treatment. The worker slipped a pair of cuffs onto his wrists. As he pulled him away, the man looked around him as though drinking in the details. His red-gray beard nearly touched his belly button.

This man wasn't just awaiting trial. He'd been in that cell for months. Maybe years.

Thaddeus shivered. In the academy there were stories about what became of agents who broke their oaths to the agency. Some said they were executed, others spoke of a prison where operatives went in but didn't come out. Thaddeus had always assumed they were nothing more than urban legends used to haze new recruits. Was it possible there was a kernel of truth to them?

The prisoner looked up and met Thaddeus' gaze. Even from a distance Thaddeus could make out the vibrant green of the man's eyes. The man's expression changed. It looked almost like he recognized Thaddeus. But that wasn't possible...

Thaddeus' throat became dry and paper-like as he tried to swallow. He turned to walk away, colliding with someone as he did so.

"Jesus!" He focused on the person in front of him. It was Jane. His face grew hot. Why was he getting so worked up? "I didn't see you," he said, his voice higher-pitched than normal.

"Mr. Broker," she said, giving him a strange look. "I hate to hurry you along, but I'm needed elsewhere." The way her eyes darted around as she spoke made Thaddeus suspect that he wasn't supposed to be in this section of the warehouse. Why not just tell him so?

"Of course."

"I truly am sorry," she said, her smile forced, like a dog expecting to be hit.

"It's no trouble at all. I was about to come find you." He looked back at the prison. "What is this place?"

Jane began to look even more nervous. "Those are very bad people. They deserve to be in there."

"Who are they? What did they do to deserve this?" Thaddeus shivered. He could think of nothing worse than being locked down here, hundreds of feet from the sunlight and surround by a hoard of magic.

"You should really ask Mason these questions." She repeated apologetically. "Sorry. Just doing my job."

"Of course," Thaddeus said, and he allowed himself to be led away.

Chapter Four

"How long have you been rooming with Randall, Dorian?" Gram asked.

"A couple of years?" Barty said it as though he was asking the question instead of answering it.

"I see," Gram said. They'd been in the living room talking for several minutes. "It's quite a pleasure to meet the man who's been keeping my April out so late." Gram glanced at the couch between them. They were separated by eighteen inches of space, each with their hands clasped together over their knees. They lapsed into an awkward silence.

"Well," Barty said with an oversized smile, "I'd love to see the house." He clapped his hands together expectantly.

April nodded. Gram probably found the request a little sudden, but she didn't care at this point. Anything would be better than this uncomfortable conversation. "Do you mind if I give Dorian a quick tour, Gram?"

Gram stood, apparently just as eager as they were to get out of the stiflingly awkward introduction. "You two go ahead. I'll call when dinner is finished."

They stood, and as she and Barty walked towards the hallway that led to the bedrooms when Gram grabbed April's arm. "Middle Eastern?" she whispered, her eyebrow raised.

April faltered. She'd forgotten she'd told Gram that detail. "I guess it doesn't show much."

Gram let go of her arm, and April followed Barty. He leaned in as soon as Gram was out of earshot.

"Why did you tell her my—his—*whoever's* name is Dorian, anyway?"

April felt her cheeks grow hot. While Barty knew about the boyfriend cover-story, she hadn't told him about the genie. "It doesn't matter, okay? I couldn't think of any other name at the time." She bit her lip. "Don't tell Dorian, okay?"

"Oh, don't worry," Barty said. "I'm never discussing this night ever again, ever. We *definitely* should have done the pizza delivery bit."

"Gram would never order pizza!"

Barty made a face. "Pizza is healthy. You have your dairy, your protein, and your meat all in one easy-to-eat slice!"

April snorted. "Your definition of healthy and Gram's are very different. Just wait until you see what she's making for dinner." She switched subjects. "Once the enchantment's in place, if anyone approaches the house meaning Gram harm, the amulet will start to heat up?"

"Not just anyone. You have to state the specific thing the subject is in danger from," Barty said. "In this case, the collectors. My grandfather's notes state that if he didn't follow this crucial step, the amulet remained too hot to handle. He hypothesized that it's because we're always in danger of something—a freak earthquake, a shelf falling over on us, slipping with a knife."

He opened the satchel hanging from his shoulder (he and Gram had practically had a tug of war match over it when he first walked in) and pulled out the grimoire and several palm-sized sachets that reeked of something strong but undefinable. He arranged them in a circle on her bed, then spoke a strange incantation over them that she didn't understand.

"The necklace?" Barty asked.

She pulled a silver chain over her head. An opal pendant in the shape of a teardrop dangled from the end. She handed it to him. One by one, he opened each of the sachets and lowered the pendant into the contents. The smell was worse when he pulled open the drawstrings, like pungent spices and mildew. The pendant wasn't going to smell like that, was it? The contents inside the drawstring were powdery and fine, like ashes.

Once he'd finished, Barty looked up at her. "We need to put one of these in every room of the house, including pantries and closets. After that the spell will be complete."

They started in her room. They left one in her closet, behind her dresser, in the bathroom, the linen closet. As he placed each sachet he repeated the same string of syllables.

In Gram's room, they hid a sachet behind her dresser where Gram wouldn't see it.

"That leaves the kitchen, garage, and basement," April said.

"Wow, you really are showing him the entire house, aren't you?" Gram said as they walked towards the basement door.

Barty, who had thrown one of the sachets behind the stove, muttered the foreign spell beneath his breath.

"What's that? Speak up, now," Gram said, raising an eyebrow.

Barty cleared his throat. "I was just saying how I love the architecture of old houses like this one," he said. "When was it built?"

"It's not that old," Gram said. "1970s, I think."

"Ah. Well, there's some features specific to the basements of houses built during that time..."

Before he could be even more obvious, April grabbed his wrist and pulled him through the door that connected the basement and garage to the kitchen. There was a small closet in the alcove that led to the garage. Barty opened it, and several rifles fell out.

"Whoah," he said. "Your grandma's packing heat."

April snorted. "My grandpa was a hunter. Deer, mostly. Gram just can't bear to get rid of them. There's no ammunition in the house."

"Ah."

Barty placed a sachet in the gun closet, said the incantation, and they continued downstairs. As they canvassed the basement level, Barty muttered, "Is it just me, or is this the most awkward situation you've ever been in?"

"It's pretty awkward," she agreed, "But I wouldn't say it's the most awkward *ever*." Dorian walking in on her and the genie in bed? Not a lot of things could top that.

They finished placing the sachets in the basement.

"Was that all the rooms?" Barty wrinkled his brow. "I still have one left."

"I thought we had them all," April said... "Unless... did we put one in Gram's closet?"

Barty shook his head.

"Crap." They walked back upstairs. In the kitchen, they made an excuse to Gram about Barty leaving his cell phone in one of the rooms.

"Okay," Gram said. "But don't take too long. Dinner's almost ready."

They padded down the hallway and entered Gram's room. It took them a couple minutes to decide where to place the sachet. It had to be a place Gram wouldn't look. In the end, April decided on the sparkly stripper heels Gram had gotten as a gag gift from one of her friends a few years back. They hadn't moved from their spot in the corner since she'd brought them home. Barty tucked the sachet into the toe of the left shoe, repeating the incantation.

"Is that it?" she asked.

"Almost." Barty repeated the incantation once more, though this time he changed a few syllables. As he finished the sentence, he pressed his hands together, and a wave of warmth spread throughout the room. Barty's eyelids drooped and he slumped forward.

With a squeak, she caught him by looping her arms under his armpits. His forehead came to rest on her shoulder, his body pressed to hers. "Barty? Are you okay?"

He moaned. Thank god.

Before she could figure out how to set him down without dropping him, Gram's voice came from the hallway. "April? Dorian? Dinner's ready..."

She must have followed the light into her bedroom, because her face appeared over Barty's shoulder.

Her eyes widened as she saw April with Barty's almost-limp body pressed against her own.

"Oh!" she said, turning away suddenly. "Sorry! I'll be... in the kitchen... dinner's ready..."

"No, it's not—" April said, but didn't finish the sentence. What could she say, really? *Sorry, Gram. We were casting a spell on the house and needed to leave a baggie of herbs in your closet?* Yeah, that would go over well. It was best that she thought they were making out.

Gram practically jogged away.

Barty opened his eyes and looked up at her blearily.

"Are you okay?" April asked.

"Sorry!" His eyes widened as he pulled away from her. "Yes, I'm fine. It's been a while since I've cast such an extensive spell, and, well... it takes a little out of you." He adjusted his clothes, as though they might have gone askew.

"Gram walked in on us," April said.

Barty's eyes widened. "Did she see what we were doing?"

"Not exactly." April explained about Gram catching them apparently making out in the closet.

Barty closed his eyes. "You owe me so, so much," he said.

"I know," April replied. "I've changed my mind. This *is* the most awkward situation I've ever been in, because now we have to go downstairs and eat with Gram."

Chapter Five

Thaddeus hated parties. Especially these inane high-class fundraiser functions. He himself preferred a good scotch consumed alone, or perhaps in the silent company of an anonymous barstool, but even that he didn't indulge in often.

Mason had called him earlier in the day, asking him to make an "appearance" at a fundraiser held by one of the agency's public partners, a man name Michael Petersen. When Thaddeus had protested, Mason had said that the perks of his new "station" required a few sacrifices.

Just another reason to try to get out of this "promotion," in Thaddeus' estimation.

"But does hobnobbing with the rich and drinking their champagne really constitute a sacrifice? No way, Jose!" Mason had then hung up the phone before Thaddeus could think of a believable excuse.

A few hours later Mason sent him a text instructing him to "smile, mingle, and *above all, HAVE FUN!*"

Now he was here, walking by a table filled with gift baskets that each had bids higher than the price of his car. He was wondering if he bid on the whiskey basket in the name of the cover company if he'd get to keep the contents, when someone knocked elbows with him.

"Excuse me," he said, putting on his best inane smile.

"Not at all," the man he'd bumped into said, and his voice made Thaddeus take notice. It was too trembly, too unsure of itself to belong to this crowd, which had been coddled since birth and didn't even consider it a possibility that they weren't deserving of any and all attention.

The man was turned slightly away so that Thaddeus only saw the back of his head at first. The man's body was thin, and not in a lipo-suction or I-have-a-personal-trainer-on-retainer kind of way. He looked emaciated. He held a plate piled with toothpicks that still had little bits of food sticking to them.

Then he turned so that his face was visible, revealing familiar, bright-green eyes.

Thaddeus' inane smile dropped away. It couldn't be... could it? The waist-length beard was gone and he was dressed in a too-large tux, but it was him all the same: the prisoner Thaddeus had witnessed being dragged from the warehouse prison. But what was he doing here?

The man's face immediately blanched upon seeing Thaddeus. He recognized him, too.

"Pardon me." the man turned before Thaddeus could respond. He was halfway through the crowd faster than Thaddeus would have believed possible for a man in his condition.

"Wait!" Thaddeus called after him. Several people turned to look at him, curious at his outburst.

He smiled as though it were a joke. "Sorry," he said. "I swear I know that man from a holiday I took once in Bosnia. If you'll excuse me, I'd really like to find him and see what he's been up to..."

He found the man again at the buffet table, where he was piling his plate with more food. He jumped when he saw Thaddeus.

"Excuse me," Thaddeus said, "Don't I know you?"

The man shook his head. "I don't believe so."

Thaddeus knew that this was the prisoner, even if he hadn't given himself away by running like he'd seen a monster. "Are you sure? I swear I saw you at a warehouse where I was conducting business the other day."

"You are mistaken." The man popped a bacon-wrapped pickle into his mouth. Though he tried to act indifferent, his eyes kept darting back to Thaddeus as though keeping tabs on a dangerous animal.

"*Please,*" Thaddeus said. "I need to know why you were in there, and what you're doing here."

The man looked away. "If they see me talking to you I'll be in big trouble."

"Who?" Thaddeus asked. The agency? The man didn't answer, so he said, "No trouble will come to you. I promise."

"Don't make promises you can't keep," the man said. "Please leave me be."

"I can't do that." Thaddeus leaned in so that his face was two inches from the man's. "Maybe I'll just start approaching people and asking your name. Eventually it will get around to whomever you're so scared of that someone's looking for you. If you won't give me answers, maybe they will."

The man blanched. "If I talk to you, will you go away?"

"You have my word."

The man closed his eyes with a sigh. "There's a cinema in the basement. Meet me there in ten minutes. And be discreet about it."

He walked away into the crowd.

The ten minutes felt like an eternity. Thaddeus kept glancing at the exits, sure that the skinny little man would try to run. Thaddeus didn't know what to do with his hands. He'd clasp them in front of him before shoving them in his pockets, before fiddling his fingers together. He felt practically electric.

He breathed out. Why was he getting so worked up over this? There was a perfectly plausible explanation, one that would make him feel silly once he found it out. He should probably just leave the man in peace... but he knew he wouldn't. If he was going to sleep tonight, he needed all the answers he could get.

When the ten minutes were up, he hurried downstairs to the cinema. The movie *Planes, Trains, and Automobile*s was projected onto a wall. He found the man hiding in the back corner. They were the only people in the cinema.

"Thank you for speaking with me," he said as he walked over.

"I have only a few minutes," the man said. "They think I'm in the restroom."

"I understand," Thaddeus said. "Who are they?"

"The Petersens, of course," the man shrugged.

The Petersens? This was their house. Obviously, Mason knew them through the front company, but Thaddeus couldn't think of a reason that they would know a criminal of magic or care about his whereabouts.

Thaddeus decided to parse that out once he had more information. "What were you doing in the warehouse?" he said. "And why are you here now?"

The man shrugged. "I was there because they caught me."

"Caught you doing what?"

"What else? Magic."

Yes, of course. It all made sense. He'd heard stories of agents who used their position to acquire magical items. If you confiscate a hoard of magic wands, who really knows if one or two go missing? It was inevitable that some agents with less scruples would take advantage of their positions. Luckily it didn't happen often, as the punishments were severe, if mysterious.

Thaddeus found himself feeling less sorry for the man. Magic-wielders used magic because it was what they did; you could barely hold it against them. Agency operatives should know better.

"And why are you here?" Thaddeus asked. "Why did they let you go?"

The man looked surprised at this question. "Because Petersen's son is about to propose to his girlfriend, of course."

Of all the things the man could have said, this one made the least sense. "What does that have to do with anything?" Maybe this man was a family friend of the Petersens? Perhaps they'd asked Mason to let him out to attend the party?

The man looked at Thaddeus as though he were an idiot. "It's a public proposal. Very ostentatious, from what's been described to me. You know how these people are—everything's a show. Been planned for months." His upper lip curled in a grimace. "The problem is, the girl's been expressing doubts about the relationship. Mr. Petersen wants to ensure that the family is not embarrassed by a refusal, so he's requested a good old-fashioned love charm."

"They're using a spell to make sure the girl says yes? That's messed up," Thaddeus said.

"Tell me about it. But the agency has made me do much worse, and the amenities can't be sneezed at." He lifted his champagne chute. "And it's long-term. I'm out of holding for a year at least, and that's if they decide to get married tomorrow—which may be the case, considering the whopper I'm about to cast on this poor girl." The man shivered and drained the glass.

"You're casting the charm?" This didn't make any sense. "Why would the agency be sending out court-marshalled agents to do cast love charms? Even if you stole a few items, you wouldn't have the experience to do this kind of magic."

"I'm not an agent," the man said. His lip curled. "Don't insult me." He pulled the collar of shirt down to show Thaddeus an iron collar around his neck. It had symbols that Thaddeus recognized quite well. They were the collars they used to bring in wielders. They both inhibited magic and forced the wearer to follow orders. They used a witch or wizard's innate magic against them, and were useless against non-wielders.

"You're a wielder?" Thaddeus asked. "Why are they holding you with the agents? Why are you even alive?"

"You really don't know, do you?" the man rearranged the neck of his shirt to obscure the metal collar, though now that Thaddeus had seen it its outline was undeniable through the fabric.

"Know what?"

The man laughed bitterly. "When I was a kid, my dad used to warn me to be discreet whenever I used magic. Otherwise, the collectors would come, take my wand and any other magical items I had, and kill me dead. It was our version of the boogey-man, you know? Except it's real." He swallowed. "But it's much worse than that."

Dark realization came over Thaddeus. "They don't kill you. They imprison you."

"Bingo."

"But why?"

"Isn't it obvious?" the man lifted his arms around him as though to offer everything around him as evidence. "They steal all of our power, but they can't use it. They don't know how, except for the most basic charms and spells. And even if they did, they didn't earn that knowledge. And the magic knows. The magic always knows."

"So what if they can't use it?" Thaddeus said. He realized he'd been saying 'they' instead of 'we.' "We don't need to. We just have to keep it locked up."

The man scoffed. "I used to think you were all complicit. But you really do believe all the bullshit lies they peddle."

"What are you talking about?"

"They sell the magic to the highest bidder." The man emphasized each word as though saying something obvious to someone very stupid. "The higher-ups get as much access as they can handle. It's like driving the company car. The excess is sold off. Now you can get pretty much anything if you have enough money—even a wizard to make some poor girl fall in love with your prat of a son."

"You're lying," Thaddeus said.

"All you have to do is look around to know that it's true. Believe it or don't—what do I care?"

"You're wrong," Thaddeus said.

The man laughed. "That's real rich, especially coming from you."

The way the man said this sent chills down Thaddeus' spine.

"What's that supposed to mean?"

The man laughed. "It's just a little hypocritical for you to persecute wielders, considering who your mother was."

Thaddeus reached out and wrapped his fingers around the man's neck. The iron collar bit into the sides of his fingers. "My mother was killed by your kind. How dare you even speak of her."

The man's eyes were the size of silver dollars. He regained his composure when he realized that the collar prevented Thaddeus from squeezing. "Was she?" he said. "They really don't tell you anything, do they?"

Thaddeus considered moving his hand up higher, but then released the man. The man's hands went to his neck, checking the finger marks that must have been forming there.

"Alan?"

They both turned towards the doorway. A woman dressed in black slacks and a white button-down shirt stood there. She was obviously a member of the household staff.

She glanced between them uneasily. "Is everything all right?"

Alan nodded, adjusting the collar of his shirt. "Just catching up with an old friend."

The woman didn't look like she believed him, but she didn't question him further. "Mrs. Petersen is looking for you. It's almost time."

"Of course." Alan turned back towards him with a sneer. "Sorry to run off, but my master calls."

He turned and followed the woman out of the room.

Chapter Six

"Andre's ex-wife called the other day," Becky said as she unpacked the contents of her brown bag lunch. "Andre's credit cards were used somewhere in South America. He really did run away. I guess I didn't know him as well as I thought."

April didn't say anything. Raoul must have made it look like Andre's cards were being used. All to draw attention away from the library itself. She still didn't like it, but she'd accepted that there was nothing she could do. She'd let the feelings of guilt almost consume her, and Rico had almost been lost because of it. She was determined to keep it from happening again. At least Becky wouldn't worry about Andre anymore.

"How's his son doing?" she asked. She hadn't heard from Rico since they'd rescued him from the mouth of the stollenwurm's lair a couple weeks prior. It would be strange for a twelve-year-old boy to stay in touch with one of his father's former co-workers, but April thought about him often.

"She said he's doing well, showing more interest in his schoolwork. Reading more."

"That's good," April said, not wanting to linger on the subject. "The heat is awfully high," April said, fanning herself. "Is the thermostat broken?"

Becky snorted. "Are you kidding? I'm freezing. The city's so cheap that we might as well be working in an icebox. I had to wear my coat during storytime this afternoon." She furrowed her brow. "Are you okay? You look... sweaty."

April continued to fan herself. The heat seemed to be concentrated at her chest. She reached into her shirt and pulled out the teardrop opal. It was so hot that she had to release it immediately, lest she burn her fingers.

Her heartrate quickened. Barty had said that the opal would only activate if the collectors were heading for the house.

Gram was in danger.

She stood, her chair pushing back from the table with a loud scraping sound.

Becky's eyebrows knitted together in a look of worry. "Is everything okay?"

"I-I have to go."

She ran out the door. She started to make her way out of the building towards the front door, but then she remembered she didn't have the keys to her car. For a moment she considered running all the way home—but that was ludicrous; it would take her at least an hour. She turned around and ran up to her office.

Every head in the Werner Room, including Randall's, turned towards her as she passed through. She ran into the office, grabbing her purse and pulling out her keys. As she made her way back downstairs, Randall and Rex appeared at her side.

"What happened?" Randall said. "Is everything okay?"

"Gram's in danger," she said, panting. When had she gotten out of breath?

"The amulet?"

She nodded.

"Let's go," he said. And they ran downstairs and out into her car. Becky was in the lobby as they passed through. She was saying something, but April didn't pause long enough to hear it.

Then they were outside. "I'll drive," Randall said. "You try to call her. See if we can't get her out of the house. Maybe the collectors aren't there yet."

They jumped into the car, Rex in the backseat. He came and stood with his front paws on the center console, watching through the windshield.

April dialed Gram's number with shaking hands. It went directly to voicemail. "Damn it!" She redialed, though she knew it wouldn't make any difference.

Once they approached the house, April jumped out of the car before Randall had even pulled into the driveway. She left the car door open and ran up the lawn to the front door. She tried the knob, but it was locked. Was that a good sign? She reached into her pocket for her keys, and realized that Randall had them.

"Wait for us, April!" Randall called as he and Rex jogged up behind her.

"The door's locked—I need the keys!"

Randall handed them to her. "Maybe they're not here yet."

She opened her mouth to say she hoped he was right but stopped herself. To say it out loud felt like tempting the gods. Her lips settled into a tight line.

"We need to be cautious," Randall said. "This could be a trap."

They walked in. "Gram?" April called. "Gram—it's me, April. Are you home?"

There was no answer. April walked to Gram's room, but it was empty.

She walked back out to the living room. Randall was checking the pantry, any place where someone might hide.

"Did you find her?" he asked.

She shook her head and walked into the living room. She gasped when she saw the door to the backyard was open. The wood where the knob had been was a splintered mess. She walked over, recognizing the circular hammer marks.

"It's Thaddeus," she said, remembering the hammer he'd used to break into the library the night she'd first seen him. "He's here. I've seen this before."

Randall nodded, the muscles in his face taut. "Do you have any weapons?"

She hurried to the stairwell that connected the kitchen, garage, and basement. She opened the closet door and pulled out two of the rifles. Randall appeared in the doorway behind her, and she handed one to him.

"Do you know how to use that?" he asked.

She shook her head. "It's not even loaded," she whispered, aware that Thaddeus might be watching them. "Gram doesn't keep ammunition in the house—but they don't know that."

Randall nodded and took the gun.

April opened the garage door and looked in. It was empty.

"Gram's not here," she said. "Her car's not in the garage." Did that mean that she wasn't here to start with, or that Thaddeus had taken her and the car?

"Well, someone's here," Randall said. He nodded down at Rex, whose head was lowered to the ground, hackles raised. He pointed to the basement with his paw, like a hound who's found a bird.

"What do we do?" April asked.

"If we go down, we might be headed into a trap."

"But if we stay up here, they might get away," April said. There were no doors to the basement, but there were windows large enough to slip through without much trouble. "What if they have Gram? What if this is our one chance to save her?"

Randall sighed, glancing at his unloaded gun. "I guess we're bluffing our way out of this."

They padded down the stairs, each holding their gun at the ready. April felt ridiculous, like she was in a first-person shooter game. This was crazy. She had no right to hold a gun. She didn't even know how to shoot one!

At the bottom of the stairs, they waited for their eyes to adjust to the dim light. April didn't dare take her hands off her gun to pull the string that would turn on the bare lightbulb that hung from the ceiling. The only light came from the open door at the top of the stairs.

Rex growled at one of the corners.

Randall snapped toward the corner. "Come out, *now*, with your hands where we can see them!"

April jumped; his voice was no longer calm and contemplative, but the harsh bark of a soldier.

Slowly, a figure emerged from the shadows. April expected Thaddeus; instead, it was a woman. She was blond and dressed all in black. A silver handgun dangled from her index finger.

"Put the gun down on the floor and kick it towards me," Randall commanded.

The woman hesitated, and Randall barked, "Do it now or we shoot!"

She did as she was told. Randall stepped on the gun to stop its progress across the floor, but he didn't bend down to pick it up.

"How many of you are there?" April asked. She wanted her voice to sound as authoritative as Randall's, but it cracked as she spoke. The woman smirked.

"Just me."

"She's telling the truth," Randall said. "If there was anyone else here, Rex would know."

April glanced down at the dog. He was facing the woman and snarling. He'd positioned himself between Randall and the woman, and April guessed that if she made a wrong move the dog would be at her neck in seconds.

"Why would Thaddeus send only one person?" April asked. "It seems risky."

"This was supposed to be a one-agent job," the woman said. "Can't have an entire squadron breaking into a residential home. It spooks the neighbors. Anyway, it's not like you need a lot of manpower to apprehend a sickly old woman. Unfortunately, your grandmother wasn't home."

The calm, blithe way she spoke was bone-chilling. April's veins filled with ice at the thought of this woman anywhere near Gram.

"My grandmother is not involved with any of this," April said.

"Oh, but she is, Pagewalker," the woman said, her black eyes flashing in the light from the stairwell. She took a step forward, testing her bounds.

"Don't you move another inch," Randall said. He cocked the gun. The woman froze.

"What do you want with her?" April asked.

"To use her to get to you," the woman said. "Obviously."

April blinked, trying not to imagine what that meant. *It didn't happen*, she told herself. *Gram is safe*. But that wasn't true, was it? Gram wasn't in their custody at that very moment, but she was far from safe. "Where were you going to take her?"

The woman didn't answer. "You're shaking," she said instead. "Are you have the brass to shoot that gun?" she took another step forward.

"Get back!" Randall yelled. Rex punctuated the command with a snarl.

"I don't think these guns are even loaded," the woman said. "Otherwise you would have shot me, like you said." She stepped forward again. "Well, at least *he* would have."

"Do you really want to find out?" April asked. She'd meant it to be threatening but even to her own ears it sounded weak.

"Might as well," the woman shrugged. She had a calculative look on her face. "If the gun is loaded, then you're just going to kill me after you question me. What do I have to lose?"

She walked up and stood next to the rifle. "But it's not loaded, is it?"

April pulled the gun back and smacked it into the side of the woman's face. The woman stumbled to the side, almost falling to the ground. She caught herself on one of the shelves lined with paint cans.

"How's that for loaded?" April snarled.

April heard a clicking sound. Randall had picked up the handgun off the floor and was now pointing it at the woman.

The woman wiped at the side of her mouth where the gun had struck her and looked down at the blood on her fingertips. She looked up at April with a predatory smile, but didn't make another move. She still held onto the edge of the shelving unit for support.

"What should we do with her?" April asked. She didn't want to see her anymore, and she wanted her gone before Gram came home.

"Sounds like a job for Raoul," Randall said. "He can question her and watch her until we figure out a better solution. Do you have his number?"

April shook her head. It was in the employee directory at work but she didn't want to say so in front of the woman—it seemed like the collectors didn't know about Raoul, and she wanted to keep it that way. She'd never thought she'd need the morning janitor's number at home, so it wasn't one of the numbers she'd programmed into her cell phone. Maybe she could call Becky and ask for it...

Before she could think of how she'd be able to simultaneously explain why she ran off and why she needed the janitor's phone number, the woman yanked on the shelf with a grunt.

The shelf and the cans of paint toppled over on Randall. All the paint cans were on the bottom shelf and the unit itself was light, so Randall was unhurt, but it was enough to knock him over. Rex dodged out of the way.

The woman looked at April for a moment, and for a second she thought she was going to attack her. Instead, she said. "I'll be seeing you—and *Gram*—very soon."

She pulled something out of her pocket. It looked like a marble. She threw it on the floor, and it cracked. As soon as it did, the room erupted into light brighter than anything April had ever seen. She shielded her eyes from it.

Shots fired—was Randall shooting at the woman? Did he get her?—seconds later, the bright light disappeared, but April was unable to see in the sudden gloom.

"Are you okay?" she asked Randall.

"I'm fine." He grimaced down at his paint-covered tennis shoes. "But she got away."

As April's eyes adjusted to the dark, she saw that he was right. "Damn it!" she kicked the edge of the fallen shelf. Streams of chalky color leaked out from the overturned paint cans and pooled on the floor.

Rex sniffed where the woman had been and whined. He looked confused.

"It's okay," April said, walking over to the dog and patting his head. "She tricked us all."

April pulled out her phone and dialed Gram's number with shaking fingers. Her anxiety mounted with each ring. After the third tone, Gram answered. "Hello? April?" she said. She sounded worried.

"Gram?" April swayed back and forth, nearly falling over as relief flooded her body. "Are you okay? Where are you?"

"Oh, you know," Gram said with a laugh. "Rita called and asked if I wanted to grab lunch. We're at a café downtown. I guess I turned my phone off." She paused, her voice suddenly suspicious. "Why? Aren't you at work?"

April steadied her breathing. "I forgot something, so I came home for lunch." She paused. How much should she tell Gram? She'd need an explanation for the mess in the basement and the ruined back door. "When I got here the back door was open. Someone broke into the house, Gram."

"*What?*" Gram said. "Are you okay? Did they take anything?"

April shook her head. "No. They're gone. The basement is a mess, but the rest of the house seems untouched."

"I'm coming home right now," Gram said.

"No!" April said. She had to get back to the library. What if the woman came back? "I think you should stay out of the house for the rest of the day in case they come back. Why don't you and Rita make a day of it?"

Gram paused. "Well, we were talking about seeing a movie... but someone has to call the police."

"I already did. In fact, they're leaving right now. They said they can't do much." She paused. "I'd really feel better if you stayed out until I come home. I'll leave work as early as possible tonight."

"Well, okay," Gram said. "If it makes you feel better. Just let me know if something else happens, okay? I'll leave my phone on."

She was already explaining to Rita what had happened when April hung up the phone.

Randall spoke. "It's lucky she was out. If she'd been home..."

"Why was that woman hiding in the basement?" April asked. "Gram wasn't here."

Randall paused before speaking. "She was waiting for her to come home, April. She must know your schedule and know that your grandmother would most likely be home before you. It's lucky that Barty's enchantment worked."

April shook her head. "Luck isn't enough! We need something better. But what chance do we have against them? They have agents and magic and guns!" She kicked over one of the paint cans that had managed to fall right side up. It spilled its contents on the floor, a sickly green color that mingled with the rest of the puddled hues.

She knew now why Mae hadn't had any friends or relatives when she died. She'd distanced herself to keep them safe. Was that April's fate? A life of loneliness?

Randall nodded. "We'll talk about it tonight," he said. "We need to get back to the library." He glanced down at his clothes. "Right after I get changed."

~~~

When April walked back into the library, Becky ran up to her. "Are you okay?" she said. "What happened? You ran out of here so fast. I mean, you were on your lunch break, so it's okay, but..."

April just stared at her. What could she say? That she'd rushed home to save Gram from a tyrannical organization set on destroying all the world's magic? But she needed some excuse...

"Someone broke into my house," she said, finally.

Becky's eyes widened, "Oh," she said. "Is your grandma okay? Did you call the police?"

"Gram's fine," April said. "Luckily she was out with a friend when it happened. I called the police when I went home. They said there's not much they can do. The person is still out there, somewhere." April pictured the woman's cold, calculative eyes. It was like staring into the eyes of a UNC, except instead of indifferent emptiness they were filled with something closer to evil.

Becky narrowed her eyes. "I see... but how did you know? Did a neighbor call you? You didn't get any phone calls. You didn't even have your phone out."

Crap. Why hadn't she thought of a better excuse? She couldn't tell Becky the truth. "I just... knew, okay?"

Becky got really close to April. The intensity in her eyes was almost frightening. Becky held her gaze for several seconds, then she placed a hand on April's shoulder. "I understand completely," she said. "As women, our intuition is one of our most powerful attributes. Moira will flip when she hears this!"

"Who's Moira?"

"My spiritual advisor," Becky said earnestly.

April didn't move for several seconds, then she nodded. "Right," she said. "I'm glad you understand. I better get back upstairs. Clara will be wondering where I am."

April walked into the Werner Room, barely noting Clara looking up at her before walking into her office. She shut the door behind her and then locked it.

Her hands shook as she dialed the phone, not even needing to look up the number.

"Hello?" Thaddeus' familiar voice drawled over the phone.

"How dare you!"

"Ms. Walker?" Thaddeus sounded surprised.

She scoffed. "Like you weren't sitting there, clasping your hands, just waiting for me to call!" she said. "How could you?"

"I honestly don't know what you mean."

"Right, because attacks on sickly old women just orchestrate themselves!"

Pause. "What happened?" he said.

He didn't sound surprised, exactly. It was more like he was wary, dreading what she would say.

"One of your agents broke into my house," April said. "She was after my grandmother."

"Did she succeed?" Thaddeus asked, his voice tight.

"No," April said. "Gram wasn't home."

There was static as he breathed a relieved sigh. "I warned you. Didn't I tell you to prepare?"

"We did," April said. "We put a spell of warning on the house."

"*A warning spell?*" Thaddeus said, disgust apparent in his voice. "That's the best you could come up with?"

Why was she the one being put on the defensive? "If you hadn't obliterated all the spell books in the world, maybe we could have come up with something better," she said.

"What good will a few moments of forewarning do for you, Ms. Walker? You were incredibly lucky today."

"I know," she said, all her anger flooding out of her. This was her fault. She hadn't prepared enough.

There was a pause at the other end of the line. "Describe the agent."

April tried to concentrate. She'd been in such a panicked state that it was difficult to recall anything specific about the woman. "She was blond," April said. "And she had these stone-cold eyes. She looked crazy, but *smart* crazy, if that makes sense. Like a lion or panther or something. Like she's capable of anything."

"Damn it," Thaddeus said.

"You really didn't know, did you?" April asked.

"No, I didn't," Thaddeus said. "And the fact that I wasn't informed of this means I can no longer protect your grandmother." He paused. "Listen very carefully," he said. "Unless they've decided to escalate, you have a day or two to figure out a plan. You need to up your game. No more of this cutesy parlor trick bullshit. *Real* magic, *real* protection. If you can't muster the magic you need to figure something else out. Got it?"

She nodded, then realized he couldn't see her. "Yes. I understand."

"Where's your grandmother now?"

No way was she going to tell him. "Somewhere safe."

"Good. I'll do what I can," he said. "But I'll be surprised if it amounts to anything."

"Thanks," she said, and then mentally kicked herself. Why was she thanking Thaddeus? This was his fault—at least partially.

"This doesn't change anything between us," Thaddeus said coldly. "You had more than enough chances to change sides. You chose your fate. But your grandmother shouldn't suffer for your choices."

"That's fair." She swallowed. "Thaddeus?"

"Yes?" he sounded tired.

"Why do you hate magic so much?"

She waited so long that she was sure he wasn't going to answer. She was about to ask if he was still there when he said, "A wielder killed my mother. I didn't know her, but... my father never really recovered from it."

"Oh. I'm sorry." What else could she say?

Pause. "Goodbye, Ms. Walker." Click.

She spent the rest of the night clutching the necklace. Thaddeus had said Gram was safe for the night, but could she really trust him?

~~~

"The warning spelling isn't enough." April said after she told Dorian and Barty what had happened. "If Gram had been home..."

Barty clutched the grimoire to his chest. He nodded. "I'm sorry. I should have pushed myself more."

Barty had bags under his eyes. Had she really been working him that hard? "You did the best you could," she said. "We'll try something else, something non-magical."

"I have an idea," Randall said. "I'm not doing anything during the day... why don't I hang around outside of your house? I could stay hidden, keep an eye on things."

Dorian nodded. "That's a good idea. Raoul might be able to help as well. I'll give him a call. Maybe he can loan you a car to sit in, at least."

"Perfect," April said. She'd feel better while she was at work knowing that Randall was watching the house. She hadn't seen the woman's gun since they left the basement, and she assumed he'd stashed it somewhere. "I'll pick up some ammunition for my grandfather's guns. Just in case."

Barty nodded. "And I'll keep looking for a suitable spell. We'll want to get more volumes of the grimoire; I'm almost done with this one."

April's phone vibrated in her pocket. "Gram's calling." She answered the phone. "Hey, Gram. How was the movie?"

"It was okay. We saw a couple, actually. I'm heading home, now. Is everything okay at the house?"

April gripped the necklace. It was warm from her constantly holding it, but otherwise unchanged. Thaddeus had said they wouldn't attack tonight. Could she trust anything he told her? What if that was a trick to get her to let her guard down?

"Everything's fine, Gram," April said. "The cops think it was some neighborhood kids. The basement's a mess, though. I'll clean it up when I get home."

April reassured Gram a little more, then hung up the phone. "She's going back to the house. I should be there when she arrives." She looked at Dorian. "You'll call Raoul?"

Dorian nodded, and Randall added, "We'll work it out, April. You go home and take care of your grandmother."

Chapter Seven

Thaddeus paced back and forth in front of Mason's office. It was all he could do to not throw the door open and storm inside.

"He's ready to see you, now," Mason's assistant said, wide-eyed, from her desk to the side of the door. She'd been watching him pace like he was a wild animal that was liable to lash out.

He didn't need to be told twice. He pulled open the door, slamming it shut behind him.

"You sent *Silvis*?" Thaddeus said. He pushed the tiny chair out from in front of the desk and planted both of his hands on the mahogany wood.

Mason's brow raised in surprise, the top of his forehead etching into two deep lines. "Whoah, Thad," he said. "I can tell you're upset. Sit down and we'll talk this out."

"*Silvis,* Mason?" Thaddeus repeated. "The woman's a goddamned sociopath—"

"*Sit. Down.*" Mason said, his voice low and dangerous. Thaddeus considered him for a few seconds, then sat down in the chair.

Mason's face returned to its normal affable resting expression. "That's more like it," he said. He walked over to the decanter set out on a small wooden table and pulled out two crystal glasses. "You want ice, Thad?"

Thad shook his head. Mason finished pouring and held out one of the glasses for him. Thaddeus took it but didn't drink.

Mason walked over to one of the windows that looked over the rolling hills of his estate. In the spring and summer it was as green and manicured as an upscale golf course. Today it was brown and dead. Not even the rich could cheat the seasons.

"You know I think of you as a beloved nephew, Thad. Your father was like a brother to me. But I am the director of this division. I have a duty to protect the sanctity of the mission. And I fear that recently your judgement has become... clouded."

"Clouded?" Thaddeus said, aghast. "I am as dedicated to the agency's mission just as much as any other agent. More so."

"Up until recently, I would have said the same. I had to see the tape for myself to believe it. I must say, I was disappointed in you, and not a little embarrassed for myself."

"What are you talking about?" Thaddeus said.

Mason took another draw from his glass, then walked over to his desk and pulled out a stack of papers. He slid on a pair of reading glasses, thumbed to a page in the middle, then began to read.

"*My superiors want to come at you with everything they have. They've decided harsher tactics are necessary ... I was able to find you here. They will, too ... They will come for you. They'll come for your grandmother, and they'll come for your friends. They will show no mercy.*" He paused, then looked up. "Need I read on, or do these words ring a bell?"

Thaddeus' heart nearly skipped a beat. These were all things that he had said to the Pagewalker at the clinic the previous week. He'd known the agency had the power to access the security footage, but they had no cause to. They were more invested in the library gate case than he'd thought.

"The cameras at the clinic didn't have microphones," Thaddeus said. "How did you get the transcript? Lip-readers?"

Mason nodded, then closed the packet and placed it on the desk. He stared at Thaddeus over the tops of his reading glasses like some disappointed teacher.

"If you have an alternative explanation that doesn't point to your utter betrayal, I'd love to hear it. This hurt my heart, son. You endangered the mission. You don't know the strings I had to pull to convince the partners that you aren't colluding with the enemy."

Thaddeus tried to hold onto the anger he'd felt earlier, but he felt himself becoming unsure. Was Mason right? Was he not seeing things clearly?

"The grandmother," he said. "You were going to kidnap her. Worse. She has nothing to do with all of this. Targeting innocents goes against everything we stand for."

Mason nodded once, then sat down in his chair. "You have a good heart, Thaddeus. It's why your betrayal cut me so deeply. What would your father think?" he paused. "I did what I could to mitigate the situation. To protect you from yourself."

"The promotion," Thaddeus said. "You reassigned me to keep me away from the case."

"Your judgement was clouded," Mason said. "I wanted to protect you from what needed to be done."

"But she's innocent," Thaddeus said.

Mason nodded sadly. "You're right. The grandmother doesn't deserve to be targeted. But what about the security guard? What about his son? The boy was almost lost. How many more will die to save the grandmother? She has months left, at best."

Thaddeus hung his head. "You're right," he said. "I wasn't thinking clearly."

Mason reached over the table and grasped his shoulder. "I'm glad to hear you say that, son. Your father would be proud."

Thaddeus' nod was only half-hearted. He took a long draw from the glass. There had to be a way to get the library portal without going through the grandmother. He just wasn't seeing it.

Chapter Eight

April and Gram were eating lunch in the food court. The few items they'd purchased—work clothes for April, mostly—were already stowed safely in the backseat of the car.

Gram picked at her stir-fried vegetables. "Do we have time to stop by the book store?" she asked. "I want to pick up the new John Grisham book."

"Sure," April said, but she had a hard time focusing on Gram's words. She suddenly felt uneasy, but she couldn't explain why.

Unperturbed, Gram continued speaking. "And maybe Anissa Stringer's new book, too..."

April wasn't listening to Gram anymore. Prompted by instinct, she reached inside her jacket and pulled out Barty's necklace. It glowed. She shoved it back underneath her clothing before Gram—or anyone else—noticed. She stood to better see over the heads of the crowd.

"Is everything all right, hon?" Gram asked.

April didn't respond, taking stock of their surroundings. The food court wasn't terribly crowded, as it was a weekday morning, but there were still a considerable amount of people around. Any of them could be collectors in disguise.

Her eyes alighted on a woman clad in an oversized hoodie with the initials of a local college embroidered on the back. The woman's head was turned away, but April couldn't take her eyes off her.

The woman turned towards her, and their eyes met. It was the woman who'd broken into the house. She'd changed her hair and clothes, but it was her.

The woman smirked, then reached inside her coat as though to access a holster. Instead, she pulled out a cell phone, like a normal co-ed checking to see if she'd gotten any new text messages.

April forced herself to look away from the woman. She scanned the crowd for other possible agents, identifying ten more people who didn't quite fit, who seemed to glance at her too often.

"Gram," she said, "We need to go, *now*."

"Go?" Gram said, confused. "I thought we were going to the book store—"

"I just remembered that I promised Janet I'd go in early today," she said. "I forgot. We have to leave now, or I'll be late."

Gram grumbled but began to rise and put on her coat. "I'll throw the tray away," she said.

"Leave it," April practically barked, and Gram looked up at her with surprise in her eyes.

"Is everything okay, hon? You're acting weird."

Unable to concentrate on Gram's words, April looked up, noticing that all the people she'd pinpointed earlier were now converging on them. Not in an obvious way, at least not obvious to Gram or anyone else. Some appeared to have seen someone just behind her, some looked like they were moving towards the trash bin to throw out their leftover food. But all of them were heading directly for Gram. The nearest one was only a few feet away, a man wearing a polo shirt and khaki shorts, his white athletic socks pulled up to his calves. He could have been anyone's dorky father.

The man reached for Gram. Without even thinking about it, April swiped his arm away. He looked surprised for a second, then reached inside his pocket. April grabbed his hand and squeezed. She wasn't any stronger than normal, so his fingers didn't break, but when she finally released (at the exact right moment, she knew) his fingers were twisted in a strange way. He grabbed his hand with the other one and screamed.

"You're crazy," he said in a lame-dad voice like he hadn't been trying to grab Gram only seconds before.

"April!" Gram covered her mouth with her hands. "What's gotten into you?" She turned to the man, apologizing, trying to examine his hand. She didn't notice that the female collector in the college sweatshirt was coming towards them, her hand on her hip. This time it was obvious she wasn't reaching for her cell phone.

A gunshot rang out, followed by screams. April scanned the crowd. Though several people had ducked down, no one appeared to be hurt. She turned to find the source of the sound.

A man stood in front of the automatic door. He was clad in a black motorcycle jacket, black pants, and leather boots. A helmet obscured his face. In his left hand he held a gun pointed up at the ceiling.

The food court erupted into chaos. Panicked screams reverberated off the walls. Some people ran, some collapsed to the floor. Some remained frozen in their seats, their mouths gaping.

A second gunshot rang out, the bullet making a ping sound as it bounced off the vaulted metal cieling. "Silence!" the man yelled. His voice was muffled by the helmet, but strangely familiar. Where had she heard that voice before? Most of the people followed the order, though a few sobbed uncontrollably. He ignored them.

He leveled the gun directly at April and Gram. "Nobody move or I'll pull the trigger."

There was something about the situation that was off. What was it?

She looked back at the man with the still claw-shaped hand and the female collector. They both looked shocked. They hadn't expected this, and they sure weren't going to risk being the ones that caused the Pagewalker to be shot. A cursory glance at the other collectors confirmed that they hadn't expected this, either.

The man in the helmet spoke to her and Gram. "You're coming with me," he said, roughly grabbing April's upper arm with his free hand.

"Ow!" April said. She tried to pull free, but his grip was too strong.

He turned back to the food court. "If anyone follows us, I will shoot them. If the police are called, I will shoot them. Understand?"

The food court remained deadly silent.

"Let's go." The man released April's arm and pushed her out in front of him.

"Come on, Gram," April said.

Gram came and stood next to April, but she didn't start walking. Instead, she put herself between the man and April.

"Run, April," she said, and there was no doubt that she was prepared to take a bullet to give April a chance to get away. She stared at the man defiantly, daring him.

"Do you want to die?" the man said, his voice frustrated.

"Come on, Gram," April said. She took Gram's elbow and started walking. The man directed them through the automatic door. They walked out to the curb, where a motorcycle was parked with the engine running.

"Get on," the man said.

Gram turned to face him. "Leave my granddaughter," she pleaded. "You only need one hostage. Take me."

The man didn't respond to her plea. "*Get on,*" he ordered again.

"We'll be okay, Gram," April said. Reluctantly, Gram allowed herself to be helped onto the bike. April sat in front of her, and the man up front.

"You can't really plan to drive this thing with all three of us on it," Gram said incredulously.

She yelped when they sped off. April realized he was driving towards her car, which was parked out towards the back of the parking lot.

During the ride, April tried to place the man's voice. She *knew* she recognized it from somewhere. But where?

Because of the roar of the engine, she saw the flashing blue and red lights before she heard the sirens. Someone inside must have ignored directions and called the police.

The motorcycle stopped a few feet away from her car.

"Get off," the man instructed. Not needing to be told twice, April hopped off and then helped Gram do the same.

Once they were off, they stared at the man, waiting for further instructions. "Drive home," he said. "The cops won't bother you."

"What?" April asked.

"*Go. Home.* Or you can go back in there and let those agents take you."

Agents? Suddenly April recognized his voice. "Thaddeus?"

She couldn't tell if his expression changed through the helmet. He kept the visor trained on her for a few more seconds before turning away and speeding off. The flashing lights followed him.

"What do we do now?" Gram asked.

"Let's go home," April said, for some reason wanting to do what he said.

She'd known Thaddeus was sympathetic to Gram's plight. If she understood correctly, he'd just sabotaged a mission to protect her. What did that mean?

Chapter Nine

April barely made it through the day waiting for the library to close so she could tell Dorian and the others what had happened that morning. It had been hard enough to calm Gram down. Luckily Gram hadn't insisted on calling anyone.

Why would Thaddeus save them? And if it wasn't Thaddeus, who was it?

She didn't spend much time on the latter question. She knew in her heart that it was Thaddeus. She wished she could explain things to Randall and ask for his advice, but he was at her house keeping an eye on Gram.

He showed up around eight fifteen.

"What are you doing here?" April said, panic rising in her chest. "Is everything okay?"

"Relax," Randall said. "Raoul showed up around seven. He'll watch the house until you get home."

April's pulse slowed slightly. She nodded. Of course Randall wouldn't leave Gram vulnerable.

"Is everything okay?" he asked.

"Something happened this morning," she said. "I'll explain after close."

He nodded. "I'm going to walk around the first and second floors, see if Becky and the others need any help." He paused. "Unless you want me to stay with you?"

She shook her head. "No. That's fine. Go ahead."

After Dorian and Barty showed up, she told the others about what had happened at the mall that day.

"Has there been anything on your news about it?" Dorian asked.

April shook her head. She'd done an internet search while on the desk, but nothing came up. Barty confirmed this, saying that the television in Nemo's lobby had been playing the local news, and it hadn't been mentioned.

It was so strange. The collectors wouldn't have reported it, but what about all the people that had been in the food court? Surely someone would have called the local news. Wouldn't the cops want to find them and make sure they were okay? The collectors must be suppressing the story somehow.

Barty looked up at her. "But the amulet worked, right? It glowed?"

April nodded. "I had it tucked inside my shirt. I didn't notice it right away."

Barty suppressed a smile.

"But who was the man who saved you?" Randall asked. "Who would want to go up against the collectors? Who would even know what they were planning?"

April hadn't told them her theory yet. "I think it was Thaddeus."

"Thaddeus?" Randall and Barty said in unison, their voices incredulous.

Dorian shook his head. "He and his father spent their lives trying to dismantle everything Mae and I built here. Why would he save you?"

"I know it was him."

"I thought you said he didn't take the helmet off," Randall said.

April nodded. "He didn't. But he spoke to us, though. I recognized his voice."

Dorian shook his head. "I'm usually wont to believe you, but considering who we're talking about, it's clear you misheard."

"That's not the only reason," April said. "I was sitting there, and I just *knew* that we were going to be attacked. I knew before I noticed the amulet glowing. I probably wouldn't have even realized it was glowing otherwise, because it was tucked into my blouse. It was like my body was reacting without me controlling it. It was the gate."

She shivered at the memory. She had felt powerful and hyper-focused, but it had been scary, too, like something had taken over her limbs. Like she was possessed. The thought conjured up images of UNCs.

"Like a spider sense?" Barty said, wrinkling his brow. "A Pagewalker sense?"

April nodded. "Something like that. I got the same feeling about the biker. I just knew it was Thaddeus." She turned to Dorian. "Did anything like this ever happen to Mae?"

He thought for a moment. "I don't think so. She'd get hunches, but nothing like what you're describing. At least, not that she told me."

"It was like I was watching myself from outside of my body."

Randall looked concerned. "Are you sure you weren't just experiencing a rush of adrenaline? A lot of people who go through intense situations describe similar feelings of disconnectedness. Their reflexes get faster and some even have improved strength."

Randall's words sounded similar to what she'd experienced, but she knew in her heart that it wasn't some adrenaline rush, like a mother who's able to lift a car to save her child. The gate was affecting her physically and mentally, and she wasn't sure if she was okay with it.

"I know what it was," she said quietly.

Randall nodded. "Okay."

They sat in silence for several minutes. Barty was the first to speak. "What now?" he asked.

"I don't think I want to work on the ink rot tonight," April said. She still felt jittery. "Anyway, I should get home to Gram."

Dorian shrugged. "That's not a problem. I'm not even sure that the books I've set aside actually have ink rot, or if it's imperfections in the printing."

"I mean," Barty said, "What should we do about this situation?"

April breathed out. Now was time to unveil her idea, but she wasn't sure how the others would react. "I think we should meet with Thaddeus. Ask him why he saved us."

The others erupted into speech simultaneously.

"You must be mad—"

"They *shot my dog*—"

"His father sent people to try and *kill* me—"

April put her hands to her temple. "Shut up!" she said, and they all fell silent.

"He can tell us what they're planning, why they're coming after us now. They came after Gram twice already. They'll try again." She clutched the opal charm, making sure that it was still cool to the touch. She'd told Gram to stay in the house, but what if she decided to go out for some reason? What if Raoul didn't see her?

Silence fell over them again. A wave of exhaustion washed over her. She needed a break, a distraction.

"Let's sleep on it," she said finally, "We'll continue this discussion tomorrow."

Randall and Barty left, and after gathering her belongings from her office, April walked out to the Werner shelves. Dorian was there with his notebook, examining the books. She pulled down *One Thousand and One Nights*.

Dorian sighed, looking away from the book on the table in front of him. "I thought you wanted to go home to your grandmother," he said.

"I will. I won't stay for long. An hour, tops." She walked towards the gate, then turned around. "Why do you care so much?" she asked.

Dorian looked up at her. "I told you, I don't care. I just thought you might like to relieve Raoul."

The fact that this reason was completely logical made her irrationally angry. "Really?" she said. "The genie says you're jealous."

She regretted the words as soon as they left her lips. Why had she said them? What would they accomplish, other than to make things between her and Dorian more awkward?

Dorian sat back in his chair. "Oh, did he?" he said, small roses of color blooming on the apples of his cheeks. "Well, I trust that you don't believe a word of it. He's just trying to get into your head."

"Of course I don't. I... I don't know why I even brought it up."

"Good."

"Fine."

He sighed. "There's no point in checking for ink rot tonight. I'll be in the meeting room watching a movie on the projector. I think we could all use some distraction."

He walked away and disappeared down the stairwell. She walked towards the gate and opened *One Thousand and One Nights*. She opened her palm, revealing the small slip of paper she'd hidden there. On it she'd written:

I grant Thaddeus Broker access to the library.

She threw it through the gate before stepping through herself.

Chapter Ten

When April left for work the following day, Gram was in the living room flipping through the local news stations. She hadn't gone out for her jog that morning, and there were bags under her eyes. The run-in at the mall had affected her.

"Can you believe it?" She said. "Not one station covered what happened yesterday. Do you think the police are trying to keep it under wraps?"

April shrugged. She'd thought about what to say to Gram about the lack of coverage. "They probably don't want to scare anyone. Maybe they caught the guy."

Yeah, right. Like the Minneapolis Police Department was capable of dealing with the collectors.

"Well, that's just outrageous," Gram said. "People have a right to know." She turned to look at April. "Do you think I should call one of the news stations?"

April shrugged. "I certainly don't want to talk to any reporters. You go ahead if you want your face all over the evening news, but leave me out of it."

She held her breath. Gram wasn't the type to want to be on television—she often made fun of the people whose faces did show up on the news. She might have been prodded into action if April actively tried to talk her out of it, though. She was stubborn like that.

"Hmm," Gram said. "You're right. I don't want to talk to any reporters, either."

April breathed a sigh of relief as she walked out the door.

~~~

Later at work, April stared down at the desk phone.

Bringing Thaddeus to the library was risky for sure. But something was going on. And somehow, with her Pagewalker sense (as Barty called it), she knew Thaddeus could help. It wasn't even a little bit logical, and it would come with consequences. But it was the best way to protect Gram.

She picked up the phone. She dialed before she could stop herself, like she was a middle schooler calling a crush.

"Hello?" Thaddeus' familiar pompous voice came through the receiver. April didn't respond right away. There was still time to hang up the phone...

"Who is this?" Thaddeus asked, sounding annoyed and suspicious.

"It's April. April Walker," she said.

"Oh," Thaddeus said. "Ms. Walker. I wasn't expecting your call. To what do I owe the pleasure?"

Not sure how else to broach the subject, she blurted, "Thanks for saving me."

"Saving you?" The words were meant to sound surprised, uncertain, but she could tell that he was wary of the call.

"At the mall. I didn't know you drove a motorcycle."

Pause. "I don't know what you're talking about."

"Do you mean about the attack, or about you saving me? Because you should at least know something about it, whether it was you on the motorcycle or not."

He didn't respond.

"Listen, I *know* you were the one who saved us. I don't know why you did, but we could use your help." She'd wrapped the phone cord so tightly around her hand that her fingers were starting to turn purple.

There was a pause on the other end. "I can't."

"Sure, you can," April said. "Come to the library tonight."

"What about the protection spell?"

"I've removed it for the evening."

"That's unwise."

She knew that for sure. But it was the only way she could think of to even have a chance at protecting Gram. "This applies to you only," she said. "If we sense another collector within a ten-block radius the ward will be reinstated before you are able to put one foot inside the door. And we have magic set up to tell if this is the case." This was untrue, of course, but it couldn't hurt to have Thaddeus think otherwise.

"What makes you think I'll come?" Thaddeus asked.

"This is the second time you've saved me."

"Warning you that they might come after your grandmother is hardly saving you," Thaddeus said, and she could practically hear his eyes roll. "You should have been able to figure it out yourself. You come from a nicer world where people won't do the unspeakable to get what they want. I was just levelling the playing field."

There was a note of regret in his voice. She decided to take advantage of it. "If you have such a moral compass, why are you working for an organization that targets innocent people without a second thought?"

"I work for the agency because magic is a dangerous abomination that needs to be contained. Collateral damage is unavoidable."

"That may be so," April said. The image of Andre on the Werner Room floor, unmoving, flashed in her mind, but she blinked it away. "But it doesn't mean you need to accept barbaric methods. Join us. Help us."

There was a long, heavy pause. "Goodbye, Ms. Walker," he said, and hung up before she could respond. She sat motionless for several seconds before she realized she still had the dead receiver held against her ear. She put it down.

Would he come? She hoped so. He was their best chance. What if she hadn't made the right decision? The last time she'd made a big decision, Andre had gotten killed.

She closed her eyes, hoping that she'd done the right thing.

Chapter Eleven

"You did WHAT?" Dorian's face was every shade of red that it was possible for a human face to be. He now looked more demon than angel. A very beautiful demon, sure, but a demon nonetheless.

"He has information we can use. He's our best shot at having even a chance against the collectors."

"We went *through* this," Dorian said. "We talked about it last night. If I remember correctly, we all said it was a terrible idea."

"He saved my life, Dorian. He saved Gram's life."

"You don't know that for sure," Dorian said. "Even he says otherwise. Why would he help us and then deny it, huh?"

"A lot of reasons," April said. "Maybe he doesn't want them to know that he helped us. Why else would he disguise his identity?"

"You've made this decision for all of us," Dorian said sulkily. "Barty, Randall, myself, blast, even *Rex*"—the dog's ears perked up at the sound of his name—"have something to lose from the decision you just made."

"You think I don't know that?" April closed her eyes. "You think I want someone else to get hurt on my watch?" She turned to Barty and Randall. "What about you two? Do you think I'm making these choices willy-nilly? That I haven't given this a lot of thought?"

Neither said anything.

She turned back to Dorian. "*You* made me the Pagewalker. I may have accepted it, but it was *you* who pushed me through the gate. *You* chose me, which means you knew that I would sometimes make decisions that you wouldn't like."

She paused, waiting for him to respond. When he didn't, she continued. "They aren't coming after me, okay? They were coming after Gram. Once they have her, they will go after everyone else I know and care about. That's basically you guys. So don't tell me I haven't thought about it." She glanced around the room at all of them. "So?"

No one spoke. They glanced between each other, and April thought she recognized something in their eyes, a mixture of sheepishness and resignation. And something else—fear.

"He may not even show up," she said. "He said he wouldn't. We're probably fighting for nothing."

"At least he has a little sense," Dorian muttered under his breath.

No one spoke while they waited. After fifteen minutes of silence, Barty stood. "I'm sorry," he said, "but I can't stay here. I've spent too much time running from the collectors to be a sitting duck now."

"I understand," April said. "We'll call you and let you know what happens."

Barty nodded. His face became an unreadable blur as he donned the cap of anonymity. He walked down the stairwell and out of the library.

April tried to continue reading the next book from Dorian's list, but she couldn't concentrate on the words. When she realized that she'd reread the same page five times without remembering anything that had happened on it, she sighed and closed the book. A few seconds later, the grandfather clock began to ring.

When its tenth chime rang out into the library, she said, "Looks like he's not coming." The idea felt almost like a relief. As much as she believed that he could help them, the others were right. It was dangerous, like inviting a fox into a henhouse.

Then, as though waiting for these words, three raps rang out from the front door, echoing through the empty library.

"Well, that's not the milk man," Dorian said, his jaw tight.

April looked at all of them. "What do I do?" she asked.

Dorian crossed his arms. "You tell us. You're in charge here, after all."

She winced. She deserved the barb. "Let's let him in."

Dorian accompanied April downstairs. Randall and Rex stayed upstairs.

Thaddeus looked mildly annoyed. "You go through all this trouble of inviting me here," he said, "and then you leave me freezing on the doorstep. I almost went home. I thought you'd finally wised up and were going to kill me."

"I wouldn't do that," April said, indignation rising in her chest.

Thaddeus raised his hand to quell the outburst. "Obviously I believe that, or I wouldn't have come," he said. He eyed Dorian suspiciously. "It's your comrades I don't trust."

"None of my friends would hurt you."

"Not with you in command, I'm sure. They listen to you."

"They wouldn't touch you even if I wasn't here," April said, but Dorian looked away.

Thad smiled. "I guess you haven't got around to reading his book yet. He's all about murder and debauchery." He paused. "That's right—the agency has access to your library borrowing history. Doing a little research for your job as Pagewalker? Unless you recently enrolled in a tenth-grade Literature class."

April's cheeks grew hot.

"April, it's not too late," Dorian said, his eyes flashing. "We can still kick him out."

April faltered. Maybe this wasn't such a good idea. Thaddeus had barely walked in the door and already he was clashing with everyone.

Thaddeus shrugged. "Whatever you decide. You invited me here, remember. I didn't ask for this."

April and Dorian shared a look. His response was perfect. If he had begged them to reconsider and let them in, or was chastised whatsoever by Dorian's threat, then that would mean he had a motive... then again...

"You saved us at the mall," April said. "You must have had a pretty good reason for doing that."

"I never said that was me," Thaddeus said. The corner of his eye twitched. "For all you know, I'm simply here taking advantage of your invitation."

"Sure," she said. She'd pry more later. Now wasn't the time. "Let's head upstairs."

Randall appeared calm when they entered the Werner Room, but his eyes never left Thaddeus. He seemed to be analyzing his movements, waiting for him to slip up and reveal his true motives.

Being raised by Gram, April felt the need to introduce everyone. "You already know Dorian," she said, "And this is Randall."

Randall stepped forward and extended his hand to Thaddeus, who took it. As he did, he said, "Corporal Washington—thank you for your service. I was in the military myself. And who's this?" Thaddeus bent down and scratched Rex's ears. To everyone's surprise, Rex whimpered happily.

"Name's Rex," Randall said. His voice softened slightly, confused at Thaddeus petting his dog, and maybe even more at the fact that Rex was wagging his tail and trying to lick Thaddeus' face.

"I've always liked dogs," Thaddeus said, then raised an eyebrow at their surprised expressions. "What? Who doesn't?"

"One of your men shot him," Randall said, only the slightest tremor in his voice.

"For which I'm truly sorry. But I can't fault the agent who fired the bullet when your dog was coming at him teeth first."

Randall nodded. "I've only seen him do that one other time. In Afghanistan Rex attacked a man on the street. He tore him up real good. I thought I was going to have to put him down—can't have dogs attacking civilians—until they found the machine gun hidden behind the man's back."

"Dogs can often sense much more than we can. I'm glad April's cleverness with the genie restored him to good health. There's a silver lining to every cloud." Thaddeus said. He gave Rex one final pat on the head and stood. "Right. So what can I do for you all?"

April crossed her arms. "I want to know why you saved me and my grandmother."

"Assuming it *was* you," Dorian muttered.

Thaddeus ignored Dorian and looked at her levelly. For a second, she thought that he would deny it again. Instead, he said, "I've always had differences with my superiors about what measures are acceptable in pursuing the mission. There are certain lines I'd rather not cross, if I can help it."

"Like targeting old women with cancer?" April asked.

Thaddeus shrugged. "The agency's mission is to protect the people of this world from the havoc that magic wreaks. If *we* are the ones wreaking havoc, what's the point?"

"No offense," Randall said, "But every soldier feels bad about killing people and doing what's necessary. Comes with the job. It doesn't explain why you're here."

Thaddeus thought about that for a moment. "It seemed like the right thing to do."

"The *right thing*?" Dorian said. "You're worried about killing innocents? What about the scores of wizards and witches you've killed? The holocaust you've raged against the otherkin?"

"Innocent?" Thaddeus said. "They're dangerous! You'd know that if magic was still allowed to roam free. All that's left is fairy stories, and you should thank the agency for your naivete. You remember your Merlins, your Flamels and your Nostradamuses. But trust me, their kind did more damage than the agency has ever done in all of its existence."

"Enough evangelizing," Dorian said. Everyone fell into a fragile silence.

"What can you tell us?" April said. "You must have come here for a reason."

Thaddeus looked at April. "The agency will keep coming after you and your grandmother, with or without my help. They've made that abundantly clear. If you remain unmoved afterwards, they will continue to target everyone you care about."

April nodded. She'd known this much already. "What can we do to stop them?"

Thaddeus looked at her levelly. "Nothing. Not really." He paused. "They have vast resources." His eyes darkened for a moment, then he shook his head. "Headquarters in every major metropolitan area around the world. Even if you defeated them now, they'll simply come after you later with more firepower. You don't have the resources to deal with the constant onslaught."

April swallowed. A slow, low-burning anger was filling her. Her eyes prickled with tears, and she blinked them back. Was there no way to protect Gram? "Then why did you even come?" she asked.

"I can give you information that might level the playing field," he said. "You cannot hope to defeat them, so you must find an alternate solution."

"What information?" Randall asked.

"How much do you all know about this gate that you protect so dearly?" Thaddeus asked.

They glanced between themselves, all thinking the same thing: they shouldn't tell him too much, lest they give him information he didn't already have. Did he know about the ink rot, for example? It was best to not say anything.

Thaddeus looked amused by their silence. "Each agent specializes in a different area of magic. Some go after witches and wizards, others after certain types of magical objects. My father led the unit that specialized in these gates. It was an honorable post. To truly eradicate magic from this world, we not only have to get rid of the gates—which are sources of vast power on their own—but we have to stop the possible flow of magic from other worlds to this one."

"But it's dangerous to bring things back through the veil," April said.

"That's only because this portal closes every night. You can bring things over as long as the portal is active, right? Well, fully functioning portals are always active. Oswald Werner was a very clever man. My father succeeded in deactivating this portal once, but he didn't know what the threshold was. Werner was able to find it and partially restore it several years later. If he'd managed to restore it fully, you could take all the magic from any world and transport it here without repercussions."

"It would also be infinitely more difficult to hide from the library-going public. What's the point, Thaddeus?" Dorian said.

"The point is that I'm probably the most knowledgeable person in the world about these gates. I can give you valuable information."

"*Like?*"

"Like the number of gates there were, their approximate locations, the names of the wizards who served as gatekeepers, what forms the thresholds took..."

"Thresholds?" April asked. This was the second time he'd mentioned the word.

"Yes, thresholds. The portals aren't bound to points in geography; rather, they're linked to objects. The portal goes wherever the threshold goes."

April glanced back at the middle window on the east wall. "So the gate doesn't exist on its own?"

"Well, I wouldn't say that."

"Where did the thresholds come from?"

Thaddeus shrugged. "We don't know for sure. The grimoires and journals that the agency has confiscated show that some wizards believe that the gates—thin spots between worlds—drifted around, never in one place for very long. But that eventually the magic fused to different objects, either by natural means, or at the hands of wielders."

"What do these objects look like?" April asked.

"Each is different. Some are large—so large they can't be moved. Mountains, boulders; those kinds of things. Those are the ones that we believe formed on their own, without human influence. Others are smaller, everyday objects. Some are so small they can fit in your pocket."

"Like what?"

"Anything."

"Do you know what the threshold is for this gate?"

Thaddeus shook his head. "If I did, I would have taken it that night you went back on your word. We were trying to locate it when you barged in. Do you know what it is?"

April glanced at Dorian. From the look on his face, he had no clue.

"I see," Thaddeus said.

April decided to address the question of what the threshold was later. "What else can you tell us about the history of this particular gate?"

"For one, it wasn't always linked to books in the way it is now. You would need keys for different worlds if you wanted to use it."

April resisted the urge to proclaim that she already knew this fact at least. "Go on."

"It was Werner himself who linked it to the books. We have all the keys in our custody, you see. The gate had been dormant for some time when he found it. The old wizard who served as its gatekeeper managed to hide it, though he perished in the process. One of my father's few failures."

"You have all the keys?" Randall asked. "I thought you destroyed all the magical items you find, unless they're useful to you. I don't see what use the keys would serve."

Thaddeus' eyebrows raised for only a second before his face again returned to an unreadable mask. "Of course. I misspoke."

Dorian snorted, and to April's surprise Thaddeus didn't engage with him.

"Where was this gate before Werner got ahold of it?" April asked. "Was it always here at the library?"

Thaddeus shrugged. "It's always been in the Minneapolis area. It wasn't at this location, though."

"Okay," April said. So that meant that the threshold was small enough to be portable. She resisted the urge to glance around the room. What could it be? A book?

"It was once in the care of a wizard named Michael Collins. He was the last wizard to serve as a gatekeeper. Unless you count yourself and the Jackson woman. And Werner himself, I suppose, though his role was more catalystic than anything else."

April thought about that. "What should we do?"

"If you're asking for my opinion, I think you should try to figure out what the threshold is. If you know that, you'll be one step ahead of the agency. It's easier to protect a small object than an entire building. You could even move it if you wanted, make it difficult for them to find you."

April bit her lip. This *was* good information, but... "How will this help us protect Gram? If anything, this will just make them need to target her *more*."

"I'm getting to that. Some members of the agency believe magic could be siphoned from the threshold and used to power spells."

"Barty could use it to put a stronger protection spell on my house!"

Thaddeus nodded. "Precisely."

April felt her hope dampen. "But how do we figure out what the threshold is?"

"That's up to you."

April glanced at Randall and Dorian. She turned back to Thaddeus. "Thank you. The three of us should talk this over now. In private."

Thaddeus stood. "Of course. Let me know if I can be of further help."

April thought for a moment. "You said that you have the locations of all the gates, and the names of their gatekeepers. Do you think you can get us a copy of that information?"

Thaddeus thought for a moment. "It won't be easy, but I'll do my best." He donned his coat and then turned towards them. "I will be in touch." He dipped his head in farewell, and then walked down the stairwell. They didn't start talking until they saw his form receding into the distance.

"I think we got some good information." April said.

"We know more now than before, that's for sure," Randall said. "Assuming he's telling the truth. Now the question is, what do we do with that information?"

"I think we need to do what he said—figure out what the threshold is so we can protect it," April said.

"*How?*" Dorian said. "Mae and I may not have known the term threshold, but we weren't stupid. Obviously, *something* is causing the gate, and we spent years searching for it, and never found anything. What makes you think we can find it now?"

April thought for a moment. She decided to ask a question she'd been wondering about for a while. "There's nonfiction books in the Werner Collection. Why haven't we had to clean up ink rot in any of them?"

Dorian shrugged. "Mae hypothesized that it's because they lead into your world. The ink rot doesn't affect your world."

"Have you ever gone into one of them?" April asked.

Dorian shook his head. "With no ink rot to clear up, there was no need to."

"Thaddeus said that this gate has always been in Minneapolis, right? Why not go back and ask the last gatekeeper?" she said.

"*How?*" Dorian said.

She stood and walked towards the bookshelves, to the few nonfiction books in the collection. Amongst the travel guides and a worn copy of *Darwin's Theory of Evolution,* she found the series of Minneapolis censuses. She brought one back and held it up for the others to see.

"Mae theorized that the reason the nonfiction books don't get ink rot is because it's the same world, right? Well, wouldn't that make entering this book the same as time travel?"

Randall's eyes brightened. "I think she may be on to something."

April went on, encouraged by the comment. "Thaddeus said that his father was the one who damaged this gate. It couldn't have been much further back than the forties."

Dorian looked incredulous. "So you literally want to *ask* Michael Collins?"

"Well, yeah. What do you think?" Why did anxiety well within her? She knew it was a good idea. Why did she strive for his approval?

"It's a strange plan," Dorian said. "There's a lot that could go wrong. Let's not get into the possibilities of breaking the space-time continuum. But it's worth a shot, if it gives us an edge against the collectors."

"It's settled, then." She glanced at her watch. "I better get home to Gram. We'll do it tomorrow night."

Chapter Twelve

April stared at the phone at the reference desk again. She'd been waiting for Thaddeus to call all day. She couldn't wait anymore. She lifted the receiver and dialed.

"I'm starting to get the impression that you like me, Ms. Walker," he said. She wondered how he'd known it was her.

"Hello, Thaddeus."

"I haven't been able to procure the documents you asked for, if that's why you're calling."

"I know. I mean, of course not," she said. "I wanted to ask if you knew the date your father partially closed the gate."

"Of course," Thaddeus said. "It was in July of nineteen forty-six."

So she had been right about the time frame.

"Why?" he asked, sounding suspicious.

"I think I have a way to figure out what the threshold is," she said. She told him about the census records.

"That is... nearly ingenious." He sounded impressed.

"So you think it will work?"

He clicked his tongue. "A lot of things have to fall in place," he said. "But... it's possible. It could work. Do you want me to come tonight?"

April paused before answering. "I don't think that's a good idea."

"As you wish. I just thought you might find my knowledge helpful."

"Of course," she said, "But the others aren't convinced that you're here to help."

"I understand. I'll stop by when I have the documents you asked for. Goodbye, Ms. Walker."

"Goodbye."

She hung up and looked at Randall, who was leaning against the reference desk. Raoul was keeping an eye on the house, leaving Randall free.

"Well?" he asked.

"He said the gate was decommissioned in July of 1946. He thinks my plan could work."

Randall nodded, biting his lip. April knew he had his doubts about Thaddeus. She couldn't blame him.

"Do you think I'm making the wrong choice?" she asked.

Randall shrugged. "You're making a calculated risk. I just hoped you've weighed the potential downsides."

She nodded. "I did."

"Glad to hear it." He stood. "I'm going to go check on Becky and the others."

She watched him leave via the stairwell, then turned to the phone. She had one more call to make before close.

"Nemo's pizza."

"Hi—can I speak to Barty, please?"

"I think he just came back from a delivery..."

There was some shuffling, and then Barty's voice came on over the receiver. "Bartholomew speaking," he said.

"Hey, Barty."

"Oh, April. Hey. I don't suppose you're calling to order a pizza."

"I wish." she said. "I just wanted to apologize for putting you in a difficult situation last night."

"I understand why you did it, but..." he trailed off. "How's your grandma doing? Is she safe?"

"She's fine." Gram hadn't left the house the previous day. She'd said she didn't feel like going to yoga, which was strange, but April was okay with it if it meant that she would be at home, safe. "Your spells have been a lifesaver, Barty. Really. If it weren't for the warning spell you put on the house..."

"Happy to help." He paused. "The only thing I wouldn't do over again is pretend to be your boyfriend."

She laughed. "That's understandable."

There was a moment of silence. She was the one to break it. "Will you come to the library tonight? Thaddeus won't be here. I have a plan. I can't talk about it now, but we may have found a way to power the protection spell for the house."

"Really? That's great news! I—" Barty stopped suddenly. When he spoke again, his voice was tense. "Are you sure Thaddeus won't be there?"

"Not tonight. I'll make sure there's a lot of notice before he comes again."

"Well, if you're sure..." The voice of the person who originally answered the phone spoke angrily. His voice was too garbled for April to make out.

"Okay, okay," Barty said. "I gotta go. My manager wants the line open for customer calls."

"Okay," April said. "So, I'll see you tonight?"

Barty breathed out shakily. "Yeah. Yeah, I'll be there."

~~~

"You're sure this is the right year?" Dorian asked.

April nodded. "Thaddeus said July 1946, so we need to go before that date. The census was conducted every ten years. The most recent census before that date was in 1940." She turned to Barty. "You got the right page?"

Barty nodded. She'd explained the theory about using the threshold as a power source. He'd said it was possible, but he'd need to do some tests to be sure. He'd been awfully quiet since. Was he still upset about Thaddeus?

"Are you okay, Barty?"

He nodded. "I'm fine. It's just... I spent years searching for other wielders. And now you guys are going to meet one, and I'm not."

"Oh," April said. "Do you want to come? Maybe Randall could stay here."

Barty shook his head. "Randall will be more useful to you over there."

April nodded. "Thanks, Barty. I promise we'll help you find someone."

"Sure." He smiled, though it didn't quite reach the corners of his eyes.

"Everyone ready?" She, Dorian, and Randall stood shoulder to shoulder in front of the stained-glass window. Rex waited expectantly in front of them.

Barty opened the book, and the crack in the window appeared. As the jagged cuts of glass receded, a bustling urban sidewalk came into view. Behind the pedestrians, shiny cars with elongated front ends and rounded headlights motored down the streets.

"I'll be damned," Dorian said. "It worked."

They stepped out onto the sidewalk. April looked back; the gate had opened in the covered entrance of a barber shop.

She took a moment to examine her reflection and appreciate the slight wave to her hair and her smart pantsuit before turning to Dorian and Randall.

"Okay," she said. "Now we just have to find a phone booth."

Dorian shook his head. "I can't believe this plan hinges on whether or not this wizard—who, let's not forget has every reason to stay hidden—is listed in the phone book."

"Hey," April said. "If it doesn't work, then we'll try something else. It's worth a shot."

He looked at her and nodded. "There's one on that corner."

They followed the direction he'd pointed in. Sure enough, a small phone booth stood there. It was thinner than the phone booths April was accustomed to seeing, and was constructed with wood rather than glass and metal. They walked over and opened the accordion door. Dorian flipped through the pages of the phone book until he got to the Cs.

"There are..."—Dorian mouthed to himself as he counted—"fourteen Michael Collins listed here! What do we do now—go knock on every door?"

"Hold on," April said. She looked down at the names. She pointed to the tenth one on the list. "It's this one."

Randall looked at her then looked down at the name, then back at her. "Why that one?" he asked.

April shrugged. "I just... know," she said.

Dorian looked at her, concerned. "It's the gate, isn't it? It's affecting you more."

"It's a good thing," she said. She desperately wanted him to tell her that it was, because if he didn't all there was left was her own dread that the gate was changing her. Where did her thoughts, feelings, and intuitions begin and the gate's end?

Dorian didn't respond.

After a moment, April responded, "Let's discuss it later. Right now, let's go pay Michael Collins number ten a visit."

They got their bearings by checking cross streets and asking passersby for directions, then set out.

As they neared the address, they noticed flyers for "Collins Distillery & Spirits" plastered on walls and fences. There was even a large advertisement painted on the side of a building that read, "Distillery three blocks ahead!" with a large arrow pointing the way.

"You don't think...?" April said.

"It looks like it," Dorian said.

They arrived at the address, and sure enough, the words "Collins Distillery & Spirits" were embossed in the arched stone above the entranceway. The building itself was unremarkable when compared to its neighbors. It was a square two-story red brick building. They entered through the door into a tasting room. Tables and booths were scattered across the room, but the centerpiece was the large polished wood bar with a mirror hanging on the wall behind it. Bottles filled with liquids of varying shades of brown lined a shelf below the mirror.

A man in his late twenties stood behind the bar. He held a rag in his hands, as though he'd been polishing glassware. "Welcome, welcome. How are you today, gentlemen? Ma'am?" he reached out and shook their hands in turn. "We don't normally have visitors at this time of day! What can we help you find? A good gin? Perhaps a nice whiskey? Are you looking for wholesale?"

"Actually," April said, "We're looking for Michael Collins. Do you know where we can find him?"

"I do indeed." the young man smiled. "I'm Michael Collins."

"Oh," April said. She glanced at Dorian and Randall. This man was too young to be the Michael Collins they were looking for. Thaddeus had described him as an old man when the gate fell, and that was just a few years away.

"I'm sorry to disappoint ma'am," the young man said, reading her expression.

April tried to smile. It wasn't his fault. "It's only that the Michael Collins we're looking for is older. It seems we've made a mistake."

"Maybe not. You must be looking for my father. Michael Collins Senior."

"Senior? There are two of you?"

"Yes, ma'am. Most people call me Junior. It's easier that way."

"Is it possible for us to meet him?" April asked.

Junior paused. "My father doesn't really deal with the public side of the distillery. He's more of a behind-the-scenes kind of man."

April thought fast. "This isn't a business meeting," she said. "We have a mutual friend with your father and promised to drop in and see him."

Junior's brow furrowed for a moment, but then he smiled. "I wouldn't want to stand in the way of a connection between friends. He's downstairs in the cellar checking on the barrels. I'll escort you."

He led them down a flight of stone stairs. The air grew frigid as they descended. April rubbed at the gooseflesh on her arms and thought longingly of her coat hanging on the peg in her office.

The stairwell opened into a cavernous cellar. The roof was curved in a half-barrel shape. Dozens of barrels were stacked near the walls. Water dripped somewhere in the darkness, and the sound echoed around them.

"Follow me," Junior said. "He's right through here..." He led them towards a small alcove. They could see movement inside.

Then they were surrounded with a cloud of foul-smelling dust with a pink tinge to it. April coughed as the dust entered her lungs. She had only moments to register that Dorian, Randall, and Rex were in similar straights before the edges of her vision began to go black. Just before the blackness closed in completely, a weathered face entered her field of vision. She took in a silvery gray beard and caterpillar-like bushy eyebrows before she passed out.

~~~

April was wakened by the sound of a dog whimpering. *Rex?*

"Hush," Junior's voice said, annoyed by Rex's growling. "The dog came out of that pretty fast."

"Dogs are less susceptible to sleep sand. It was alchemized to affect humans, not animals." The second voice was an older, gruffer version of Junior's. It must have been the voice of Michael Senior.

April stifled a groan. Her pulse pounded feverishly behind her eyes, her head throbbing with every beat. She felt like she was having a bad Nyquil hangover, and was glad for the cool darkness around her. The headache was so strong that it almost masked the dull ache in her shoulders. She tried to pull her arms forward to a more comfortable position and found that her wrists were tied together behind her back.

She woke up quickly after realizing this fact. She looked around, careful to move only her eyes, lest she alert the men and they knock her out again.

Dorian and Randall leaned against the wall next to her. They were tied up, too. Judging by their slumped posture they were still unconscious. Whimpering drew her attention to a wooden crate across from them—Rex must be inside. Where were they?

She forced herself to push away the panic roiling in her gut. She held her breath, focusing on her surroundings. The air was cool and damp, and she could hear the rhythmic dripping of water—they were still in the barrel cellar.

What happened? It was mere seconds from the time that she and the others were led downstairs before the powder was thrown in their face. They'd obviously found the wrong Michael Collins—two of them—but why had they attacked them? It didn't make sense...

"How did they find us?" Junior said. "I thought you warded the building from the collectors!"

Collectors? If they knew about the collectors, it meant they were in the right place. So why had they tied them up?

"I did," the gruffer voice said. "They broke through them somehow."

Randall groaned next to her, the sound loud enough for the Collins to hear. "They're waking up."

Footsteps approached, and then the two men's faces were inches from her own.

"The girl's awake, too."

Cool hands hauled her into a standing position—Randall and Dorian, too, though Dorian was still unconscious and Randall hadn't come to enough to be able to support his own weight yet.

The old man pointed a tapered stick in Randall's face. "How did you find us?" he demanded.

April realized that they were focusing on Randall because she was a woman. She fought the swell of indignation rising within her and remained quiet. Perhaps it was best to pay attention to them when they weren't paying attention to her.

Randall still hadn't fully woken up. He moaned. "Where's Rex?"

Junior shook him. "How did you find us?"

"We looked in the phone book," Randall said. April couldn't tell if he was being cheeky on purpose or if the sleep sand hadn't fully worn off yet. Their captors took it as the former, though.

"Do you think this is *funny*, collector?" Junior said. "We have you and your friends tied up—"

"We're not collectors!" April exclaimed.

The younger man looked at her, his lip curled. "Don't try to fool us. Who else would come here? Who else would know about the gate?"

"I'm the Pagewalker," April said.

"Pagewalker?" they looked at each other.

Of course, they wouldn't know what a Pagewalker was—such a thing hadn't existed in 1940.

"I'm a..." what was the word?... "gatekeeper," she said. "Like you."

"Nice try," the senior Michael said. He'd taken the stick—which she now realized was an honest-to-goodness magic wand—and pointed it at her instead of Randall. "All the gates have fallen. There are no other gatekeepers left, except myself."

"I... I know," April said. "I'm from the future."

"The future? That's ridiculous!"

"If you untied me and my friends and stopped waving that thing in my face, I might be inclined to explain," April said indignantly.

The two men looked at each other. "Do you think she's telling the truth?" Junior asked.

"I... I don't know. They certainly aren't acting like collectors. Have you ever seen them travel without weapons? Or with a dog?"

"There are two amulets around my neck," April said, grasping for any proof that they were who they said they were. "Collectors hate magic. Would one of them wear one of these?"

Carefully, the younger man pulled at the chain and string around her neck, revealing Barty's ugly stone and the teardrop opal.

With a suspicious eye in her direction, the older wizard trained his wand on the necklaces for a split second. "Basic warning charms," he said, "and weak ones at that. I don't know about collectors hating magic, but they sure wouldn't deign to wear something so weak or unattractive. No offense. Then again, neither would any self-respecting gatekeeper."

April thought quickly. "Things are... different in the future."

The old man looked her straight in the eye. "Miss, I'd love to believe your story, because it would mean that the gates have been restored. But it's not possible." He turned to his son. "Lock them up. We'll get the information out of them."

"Wait," April said. "I haven't been the Pagewalker—gatekeeper—for very long, but the gate changes you, doesn't it? It becomes part of you. Would a collector know that?"

The old man turned to look at her. He stared her in the eyes for several seconds.

"What is your gate telling you?" she asked.

The man held her gaze for what felt like an eternity. Then he lowered his wand. "Bring them upstairs, son. Make them comfortable, but don't untie them."

Junior's brow furrowed. "You believe them?"

Michael's eyes never left April's face. "I don't know yet."

~~~

Upstairs they were deposited in a small sitting area. They lived above the distillery, April realized. Randall kept looking at the stairwell anxiously. The Collins' had refused to free Rex. April couldn't blame them after the way he'd been growling and snapping from inside the crate.

April's hands were tied, so she leaned over and nudged him with her shoulder. "We'll get him back. Don't worry."

Randall tried to smile, but the skin around his eyes didn't crinkle. He wouldn't be the same again until Rex was back at his side.

"So, tell us your story."

Dorian had woken up grumpy, his face puffy and lopsided where his cheek had rested on his shoulder. She tried hard not to notice how it barely diminished his good looks. If anything, it made him appear more rugged.

April told them about the library gate, the story of how she became the Pagewalker, and about Mae and Oswald Werner.

The Collins listened to her with rapt attention. When she finished the story, Michael spoke.

"This is... great news," he said.

"It is?" April asked.

"Of course, it is! Every day we fight a losing battle to protect this gate, fearing I am the last gatekeeper, not knowing if my son will get the chance to take up the mantle in my stead... and here you are, proof that at least one other gate will reopen in the future."

April's brow furrowed. She hadn't mentioned that her gate and theirs were the same, only separated by over sixty years of time. "But—"

Michael waved his hand. "I understand that the gate isn't working to full capacity, but knowing that it's possible, even in a limited way... well, that gives me hope."

She couldn't let him go on believing that. It was like giving someone false hope. She opened her mouth to correct him, but Dorian spoke first.

"We're glad to be bearers of good news," Dorian said with a smile. He nudged her knee with his own, and she got the message: keep quiet. But why? What benefit could they get from keeping the truth from them?

Michael walked over to Dorian. "And you come from one of these book worlds?"

Dorian nodded. "I never met Oswald Werner, but I worked closely with Mae for many years. She knew very little of your ways, of course, but she did her best to protect the gate."

Michael nodded and turned to Randall. "And what stake do you have in all this?"

Randall shrugged. "I'm just a homeless guy who hangs out at the library. Can I have my dog back now?"

Ten minutes later Rex was happily sitting at Randall's feet. He recovered quickly, considering he'd woken up in a box.

While the Michaels were off fixing sandwiches, April leaned in towards Dorian and Randall. "Why can't we tell them our gate *is* their gate?

"You heard what Thaddeus said—the last gatekeeper died protecting it. Do you really want them to start asking questions about what they're doing in the future? Do you want to be the one to break that news to them?"

April hadn't thought of that. "I suppose not, but... I don't know if lying is any better."

"What if they get doubts about the mission and falter?" Dorian said.

Randall squinted. "I dunno," he said. "If you look at it like any other book, there's no mention of whether or not we were there and told them. It could go either way. Maybe we're *supposed* to tell them."

"In either case," Dorian said, "I'd rather not tell them. That way they will still have hope. There's nothing worse than knowing the future and being powerless to change it."

April glanced at him. Was he thinking about his own impending dark future, the one that he couldn't stop or escape from?

The Michaels came back with the sandwiches, and she was forced to put the thought aside. After they'd eaten, Michael said, "You didn't come all this way just to chat. What do you want from me and my son?"

Randall and Dorian both turned toward April. She finished chewing her last bite of sandwich awkwardly and then cleared her throat. How was she supposed to ask about the threshold without letting on that their gates were one and the same?

She got an idea. "We're working with the... future keepers of your gate. Tell me, do you know what form your gate's threshold takes?"

The Collins looked confused for a moment. "If you're working with our gate, then you should know Junior... or at least his descendants."

Oh, shit. April hadn't thought about that. She opened her mouth but no sound came out.

Dorian spoke up. "It's best not to discuss any details about the future. Timelines are fragile, as I'm sure you're aware."

Junior seemed to accept this, but Michael still looked suspicious. He met April's eyes, holding her gaze until she was forced to look away. "I suppose that's sensible," he said, but April could tell he wasn't convinced.

"So... your threshold," April said. "What does it look like?"

"The current operator doesn't know?" Michael asked, his eyes narrowing.

"Pop, they already said they can't talk about the future. Don't push," Junior admonished his father. He turned to them. "It's probably easiest to show you."

They were led back down to the cellar. April shivered at the memory of having the sleep sand thrown in her face. She told herself that the Collins were on their side now, nothing to be worried about. Still she checked around every corner before turning on it.

The Michaels led them to the furthest reaches of the cellar. The far wall was lined with barrels.

"I thought the gates were open indefinitely?" she asked. There was nothing the slightest bit gate-like about this place.

"They are," Junior said. He walked over to a hand crank set into the wall and began to turn it. To her surprise, the stack of barrels against the back wall split and opened; it was being retracted *into* the walls of the cellar.

"Careful," Michael said. "Some of those barrels have been there for years."

As the false wall receded it revealed an abyss of silvery, gently billowing clouds. It wasn't like any world April had seen through the veil because it wasn't a world at all. No people, no buildings, not even any ground—just endless mist.

"What is this?"

"It's what the gate leads to if the location key isn't activated," Junior said.

Michael sighed. "I haven't seen the gate in years. I'm surprised that false wall still opens, to be honest."

"You mean you don't regularly walk through the veil?" April asked.

Michael shook his head. "I understand you have to go in regularly to deal with this 'ink rot,' but for us, gatekeeping is mostly passive. We're guardians more than anything else. Seems you'd know that from your interactions with this gate's 'future operators.'" He paused. "Don't worry. I'm not asking you to spill the beans."

"Pop," Junior said through his teeth. "Don't."

"The threshold?" April asked, desperate to change the subject.

Junior pointed to the top of the arched ceiling supports that formed the gate's edges. "There. The brick at the top."

April leaned in. There was a small plaque attached to the center-most brick. In brass it read, *Collins Distillery & Spirits 1859.*

"That was one of the first stones laid when my grandfather built this distillery," Junior explained. "That brick *is* the threshold."

"I see," April said. "Give us a moment."

She drew Randall and Dorian away into the corner. "That brick looks an awful lot like the brick behind the stained-glass windows in the library," she said.

"To be fair," Randall said, "Half of Minneapolis was built with that kind of brick."

"Yeah, but half of Minneapolis doesn't open up portals to other universes at night," April shot back.

"Fair point."

"So you think that brick is what Oswald Werner found and used to bring the gate to the library?" Dorian asked.

"Seems likely."

They walked back over to the gate. Junior was cranking the wheel, and the wall of barrels closed back over the pearly white clouds of the gate.

"I hope you found what you needed," he said as they approached.

"Yes," April said. "I think we did. We should get back. Thank you for your help."

Dorian and Randall echoed her thanks.

"Don't mention it," Michael said. "Us gatekeepers have to stick together. It's too lonely of a job otherwise. It's good to have family. And friends."

April glanced at Dorian and Randall. She'd never thought about what it would be like to do this job by herself. "Yeah, it is."

When she looked back, Michael was watching his son, who was adjusting the barrels that had shifted when the wall moved. The muscles in his neck stuck out like cords. He turned to her. For a second she thought he was going to ask her about the future of the gate again. She prepared herself to lie, to feign ignorance. He opened his mouth, then closed it. When he spoke again, he said only, "Good luck, gatekeeper," before walking over to his son.

Chapter Thirteen

"What's going to happen to them?" April asked as they walked back to the barbershop where the gate was located.

"I don't know," Dorian admitted. "Mae never mentioned it. I don't think she knew, herself."

"Best guess."

Dorian sighed. "Judging by the collectors' track records, they probably took all of their magic and then executed them as soon as they were no longer worth anything to them."

"We should have told them the truth," she said. Then a dark thought entered her mind. "I let someone who thinks this is okay into the library."

"Your plan has worked so far." This was delivered begrudgingly.

Through the windows of the barbershop, April saw several men settling in for a shave. She wondered how they had gotten past the gate and hoped she wouldn't be finding a plethora of confused, scruffy men wandering around the library.

As they approached the veil, April was surprised to see that Barty wasn't alone—Thaddeus leaned against the table with his arms crossed. He held a thick folder in his hands.

Barty clutched his elbows, and his skin shone like he was sweating heavily.

Randall stopped when he saw him. "What's he doing here?" he said.

"He's holding a folder," April said. "Maybe he got the names we asked for."

"I don't like it. He should have called first." Dorian's eyes narrowed. "Are you getting any bad vibes?"

April shook her head. She hadn't gotten any intuitions from the gate about Thaddeus. She should have, if he was up to no good, right? "I think he means well," she said. "But he shouldn't be here."

Dorian nodded reluctantly, and the four of them stepped through the veil.

"What are you doing here?" April said.

Thaddeus held out the folder. "I was able to get those documents you asked for sooner than I anticipated."

She crossed her arms, not taking the folder. "You should have called before coming here. I told you not to come tonight."

"I thought you would want these as quickly as possible. I see that I've over-stepped my bounds. I'm sorry."

April considered his words. He shouldn't have shown up at the library. But he meant well, and her intuition was silent on the matter—at least the intuition that came from the gate. She took the folder.

"Just don't let it happen again."

Thaddeus nodded. "Of course. So Barty here filled me in on what you guys were doing. Any luck?"

April glanced at Barty, surprised that he'd even spoken to Thaddeus. Why was he still here, anyway? She would have expected him to leave.

Barty stared down at the table, his skin white and his neck tense. He really was afraid of Thaddeus.

Apparently, she took too long to respond, because Thaddeus said, "I understand if you don't feel comfortable sharing. I just thought that I might have some useful insight. It's why you reached out to me, after all."

April thought for a moment. "It's fine," she said. "It worked. We found out what the threshold is."

Barty grimaced from his spot at the table. April felt guilty. She'd promised him Thaddeus wouldn't be there. He must have been too scared to just stand up and leave. She'd make it up to him somehow. Maybe she'd get the Collins to come visit him.

"You can go, Barty," she said. "Thanks for sticking around, but we've got it from here."

He didn't move. He didn't even respond.

"Can you believe that the last gatekeeper of this gate distilled whiskey?" she said, trying to lighten the mood.

"I'd heard that," a voice from the stacks said.

April jumped and turned towards the voice. A man dressed in a polo and golf shorts walked out from the shelves. Behind him were several armed agents. The blond woman who'd broken into April's house stood to the man's right. "In fact, I think I have a bottle or two stashed somewhere in my office. Thad's father gave them to me as a gift. That was years ago, now. It'll be strong stuff. It's not really my brand, but maybe we'll open one. I can think of no more fitting an occasion to celebrate."

"Thaddeus," April asked, her heart sinking, "What is this?"

"Oh, of course Thad hasn't mentioned me," the man said, touching his forehead as though he'd just realized he'd forgotten to close the garage door. "My name is William Mason. I'm his boss."

His boss? April ignored the man, looking instead at Thaddeus. "What's going on?"

Thaddeus looked away. "It was the only way to keep them from going after your grandmother."

"I thought you wanted to help us!"

"I wanted to protect an innocent life."

Mason laughed. "That's Thad for you. Always worrying about the little people. If I had it my way, good ol' Gram would already be in our custody. But Thaddeus thought of this plan, and I thought, well, if he wants to go through all the trouble to set it up, who am I to stop him?"

"What is he talking about, Thaddeus?" April asked.

Randall spoke. "It was a setup, April."

"Well, it wasn't all quite planned out from the beginning," Mason said. "You see, saving you and your grandmother from the big, scary collectors at the mall was the beginning. He thought he could get in your good graces, make you believe that he was turning to your side. We never expected you to call him back and invite him in with open arms the very next day! We had to improvise, but you know what they say: when opportunity comes knocking, you open the door."

"You..." April said to Thaddeus. Unable to find a word that correctly described her sense of anger and betrayal, she finished with, "ass! You lied to me!"

Mason laughed. "Come now. There's no reason for that kind of language. If you were my daughter I'd spank you."

April gagged.

"Now, I'm going to make this easy for you," Mason said. "Agent Silvis, would you be so kind?"

The blond woman stepped forward and placed the barrel of her gun against the back of Barty's head. Barty made a sound that was a cross between a cough and a squeak. He looked like he was about to be sick.

"Tell us what the threshold is or she pulls the trigger."

"Barty, I won't let them hurt you," April said, trying to keep him calm. She turned to Thaddeus. "You're okay with this?"

Mason laughed. "The boy's a wielder. Thaddeus would trade places with Agent Silvis in a heartbeat."

April looked at Thaddeus. He wouldn't meet her eyes.

"So, what'll it be?" Mason asked. "Will you tell us what the threshold is, or does Agent Silvis get the pleasure of splattering your friend's brains across the hardwood?"

Barty looked close to tears. "It's okay, Barty," April said, hoping to reassure him. She looked back at Mason. "The threshold is a brick. One of the first laid in the distillery."

"You'll have to do better than that," Mason said. "How can we tell one brick from the myriad in this building? What do you think, Agent Silvis? Is her answer satisfactory?"

"No, sir," the woman said, and cocked the gun, her eyes glittering hard diamonds.

Barty gagged and let out a sob.

"Wait!" April raced to remember any details, her eyes never leaving Barty's face. "It has a plaque on it. It says the year the Collins distillery was founded. We think it's the brick that's right above the center of the window. It would explain why the gate materializes where it does."

"I'll be damned," Mason said. "No wonder we never found it—it would have looked just like any other brick in the rubble. Taking down gates is messy, you know." He approached the gate, squinting at the brick above the window. "Doesn't look like much," he said. "but maybe the plaque is on the other side. We all know that magic can be found in strange places. Isn't that right, Barty?" He clapped Barty on the shoulder, then reached out for Barty's hat, which rested on the table in front of him.

"A cap of anonymity! I haven't seen one of these in ages. My, this brings back old memories." He handed the cap to one of the collectors behind him before turning back to Barty. "You are under arrest for possession of a dangerous magical object." He nodded to the nearest collectors. "Take him in."

Three of the collectors approached him, one pulling out a strange metal collar from a pack of supplies.

Barty's eyes bugged out from his head. He stood, backing away from the men, but they grabbed his arms. "No, no, no, no no—" he repeated the word in panicked succession. He fought, but it was no use. As soon as the collar clicked shut around his neck, his body relaxed and he stopped fighting.

"No!" April yelled. "Leave him alone! He doesn't have anything to do with this!" More collectors approached her from the sides, each brandishing a gun. She was forced to move back.

She watched helplessly as the men grabbed Barty's arms and led him away. Barty followed them easily.

Though the collar seemed to make Barty physically complacent, it didn't affect his mouth. "I warned you," Barty yelled at her, his eyes popping out from his head in fear and rage.

"Don't worry, Barty," April called after him. "We'll get you!"

Mason made a tsking noise with his tongue against the roof of his mouth. "Don't make promises you can't keep. You're not in any better position than he is. But we'll get to you later."

Mason picked up the census records from the table. "Using the census to go back in time. It really is ingenious. I do wish you'd accepted our job offer—we could have used someone as resourceful as you. Now, back in the gate you go."

"What?" April said.

"You and your friends need to go back in the gate so we can be sure you don't cause any mischief like you did last time. Oh, and your little dog, too. I've always wanted to say that."

None of them moved and Mason sighed. "You're not going to make this easy on yourself, are you? Agent Silvis?"

Silvis approached them slowly. The gun in her hands was the only thing stopping April from slapping the grin off her face. The other goons also stepped forward.

Rex snarled at the nearest man, but Randall grabbed his collar and pulled him back, obviously afraid that he might get shot again.

April felt herself cross back over the veil. Randall and Dorian were inches behind her.

"And remember—if you aren't here when the gate becomes inactive, it's the rest of the world that will pay the price."

"Thaddeus," April called to him desperately, "You can stop this."

"He couldn't, even if he wanted to," Mason said, and with that, he closed the census and the gate disappeared behind them.

Chapter Fourteen

I should be thrilled, Thaddeus thought. His father's legacy was almost complete; the last gate was almost taken care of. *But why can't I shake the feeling that something's not right?*

He didn't like feeling this way. This was his *job,* after all. Ridding the world of magic.

But he wasn't really doing that, was he? He was just taking it from one group and giving it to another, more powerful one. A reverse Robin Hood.

He shook his head. That probably wasn't true. Alan, the "wizard" he'd encountered at the Petersen fundraiser, had most likely lied to him. Thaddeus' name must be infamous amongst the prisoners in the warehouse prison. Any of them would have jumped at the chance to get under his skin. And Thaddeus had let him. If only his father knew...

But what had he meant, calling Thaddeus a hypocrite? He'd sounded dead serious. And that comment about who his mother was...

Thaddeus excused himself from the scene in the library—Mason was setting up a magic detection spell so he wouldn't miss him—and walked down the hallway and entered one of the private study rooms down the hall.

He pulled out his phone and dialed the Petersen's home number, which Mason had given to him before the fundraiser. After a few rings a woman answered.

"Hello?"

"Mrs. Petersen," Thaddeus said amiably. He introduced himself as an friend of someone he knew her husband did business with. "I hate to call you at home, but I was a guest at your party last weekend and I really hit it off with your cousin, Alan. I forgot to ask him for his number, but I thought I'd call and see if he'd be interested in joining me for a drink tonight."

"You... want to talk with Alan?" Mrs. Petersen asked. She sounded wary.

"Yes. He's still staying with you, is he not? Again, I do apologize for calling you on your private line."

"Oh, of course," she said. "It's no trouble at all. Let me see if I can find him..." there was some scuffling on the other end. Thaddeus imagined her walking around that gigantic house. Of course, she wouldn't want to let him talk to

Alan, but she wouldn't want to risk angering one of her husband's business acquaintances.

"Here he is," She said. Before she could hand off the phone, Thaddeus said, "Congratulations on your son's engagement, Mrs. Petersen. It's obvious that they're very much in love."

"Thank you! That's so sweet!" She said, no trace of shame or irony in her voice.

Seconds later, a familiar, trembling voice came on the line. "H-hello?" Alan said.

"Alan, it's your old friend from the party. Remember how we bonded over our shared love of *Planes, Trains, and Automobiles?*" He lowered his voice. "You better play along, Alan, or they'll find out what you told me. Then it's back to the warehouse for you."

There was a pause on the other end. "Oh, yes, of course I remember. You'll have to forgive me. I had a little too much champagne that night."

"Are they with you?" Thaddeus asked.

"Yes, my cousin is right here. She's curious about the identity of my mystery friend."

"Well, I thought we could meet for a drink tonight," Thaddeus said loud enough for Mrs. Petersen to hear. "My treat, of course."

"Oh, I really don't know if I can make it. I believe I have a previous engagement tonight."

"Oh, come now. After tonight I'm flying away on business. I'll be out of the country for an entire month. Surely you can come out and share a drink with me."

Thaddeus could hear whispering on the other end. Mrs. Petersen must be urging him to accept the invitation.

"Oh, tonight?" Alan said. "I was thinking it was tomorrow. Yes, I'm free tonight. When shall we meet?"

"No reason to bother yourself," Thaddeus said. "I'm heading over to pick you up now."

Thaddeus hung up his phone. Mason and Silvis were setting up the supplies for the detection charm. He had an hour, maybe two, to kill. He preferred not to be around for the magical goings-on, anyway.

Maybe he'd finally get some answers.

~~~

"Are you actively trying to ruin my life?" Alan said. He took a large gulp from the wine glass in front of him. "Oh, god, this wine is wretched."

"If I knew your tastes were so fancy, I would have gone somewhere more high-class. I suppose your time with the Petersens has changed you."

"You know what? Screw you." Alan spat at him. "The first break I've had in nearly twenty-five years and you're doing your damnedest to ruin it."

"You've been in the warehouse for *twenty-five years?*"

Alan rolled his eyes. "They don't let us out for good behavior, mate." He drained his glass and held it up with raised eyebrows at the bartender. When he saw the look on Thaddeus' face, he said, "Oh, come on. You're going to get me thrown back into that hell-hole. The least you can do is buy me another drink."

Thaddeus sighed and raised his own whiskey glass at the bartender.

Once their drinks had been refilled, Thaddeus said, "I need to know what you meant by what you said about my mother."

"Oh, no," the man said. "I've gotten myself into enough trouble as it is. I shouldn't have said anything."

He lifted the wine glass to his lips, but Thaddeus reached out and grabbed his wrist. "You will tell me," he said, his voice low, scary. He let go after a few seconds and turned back to his glass. "First of all, how did you know my name?"

Alan sighed. "When you saw me in the compound, they were pulling me out. As you can imagine, they couldn't give me to the Petersens in the condition I was in. They want people like the Petersens to believe that we're being treated at least as well as their pets are." He scoffed. "Rich people. Totally fine with profiting from the suffering of others as long as they don't have to see it."

"Go on."

"Well, there was a bit of a fuss as they pulled me out. I heard the guards talking. They said you were there, and that you weren't supposed to be. They kept saying, 'he can't be this far in.' Got a terrible crick in my neck when I heard your name. The infamous Thaddeus Broker shows his face at the compound." Alan snorted and took another sip of his wine.

"What do you mean, infamous?" Thaddeus asked.

Alan sighed. "Are you sure you want to hear this? You seem somehow okay with the career path you've chosen. Sure you want to jeopardize that peace of mind?"

"Just tell me."

"You asked for it." He paused. "What do you know about your mother?"

Thaddeus hadn't thought about his mother in more than passing since he was in his teens, at least. She was dead. What was the point of dwelling on a woman he'd never known and never would? "She died soon after I was born. A wielder killed her. What else is there to know?"

"What proof do you have of that?" Alan said.

"What are you getting at?"

Alan sipped his wine. "She was brought into the compound before my time. She died before I was there, too. But that didn't keep her story from spreading, cell-to-cell from the cracks in our walls and the slats in our doors. We make the time go by any way we can. She became something of a legend, a story we'd tell to keep each other's hopes up."

"She was brought where? What are you talking about?"

"She came in screaming the name of her child, telling anyone who knew who her son's father was and that he'd be coming for her soon. Well, he never came for her." He leaned in close, and Thaddeus could tell he was enjoying himself. "And you want to know what the name of the child she kept calling was? Yours. *Thaddeus.* That's how I knew it was you. How many Thaddeuses do you think there are walking around nowadays? Not many."

"You're lying."

Alan scoffed. "Lying would do me no good. And that's not the end of it." He took another drink.

"A kindly woman was in the cell next to mine when I was first brought in. She used to know your mom. She said that the last thing your mom ever did with her freedom was put a powerful protection spell on you. Magic like that's usually attached to an object, but she cast it directly on you. It took a toll on her mind. All to protect you from the people you now serve." Alan snorted. "I used to feel sorry for you, you know. The charms of a hedgewitch stand no match against the power the collectors have amassed. Then we started hearing your name in a different context: as the one who was putting us inside."

"That makes no sense. If what you're saying is true, why would the agency hire me? Why would Mason take me under his wing?"

Alan shrugged. "Where better to keep someone who has the power to hurt you then right under your control? Keep your friends close and your enemies closer, right?"

Alan nudged Thaddeus with his elbow. His face was ruddy, the wine starting to take effect.

Thaddeus flashed to the conversation where Mason had told him to offer the Pagewalker a job. Was that what he was doing? Trying to keep her under his thumb?

He stood, throwing some money on the bar. "That's for the tab, and cab fare home."

"Hey, you wanted to know." Alan scooped up the money and motioned to the bartender for another. Thaddeus fled the bar. What a waste of time. He should be back at the library helping Mason complete his father's work.

It couldn't be true. Could it?

Chapter Fifteen

"They can't leave us in here indefinitely." Dorian said. "If the gate closes at five and we're still here..." he trailed off. Everyone knew what he meant.

With no other options, they'd returned to the distillery. They again sat in the Collins' sitting room, a flight of spirits almost untouched in front of them.

"Are we sure that's the case, though?" April said. "I mean, we're in the same universe—book, if you will—just several decades in the past. Does it still create an imbalance?"

Dorian shrugged. "It's possible, but the collectors won't risk it. We shouldn't, either. When they come to get us, we should be there."

April nodded. "You're right."

Junior stood. "So we wait for them to come, and then fight them."

April shook her head. "No. They'll be expecting that. They'll have all their guns trained on the gate. We won't stand a chance."

"So we get more firepower ourselves," Junior said. "We don't have any other options."

"He's right," Michael said. "The time differential between this world and yours gives us some time to prepare. We'll be ready."

"I can't ask you to do that," April said. "This isn't your fight."

"Like I said: us gatekeepers got to stick together."

Junior stood. "I'll go check our weapons stores."

"Like guns?" Randall asked.

Michael grinned. "Better. Magic." His smile faltered slightly. "There isn't much left. The collectors take whatever they can get their hands on, and there aren't many alchemists left to make new objects." He stood as well. "I'll be in the cellar. Maybe the gate has something to say on the subject. Come on, Junior."

Once the Collins had left, April turned to Randall and Dorian. "I don't like this."

"What else can we do?" Dorian said. "Just let them take the threshold? They may already have it in their grubby little clutches."

April struggled to explain. "It feels... wrong."

Dorian looked away. "April, I say this as kindly as I can muster, believe me. But your intuitions thus far have proven incorrect."

Randall looked her in the eye. "He's right, April. Our best chance is to fight."

"They'll expect that," April said. "It will be a slaughter."

Rex whined, and she patted him on the head. Poor dog. He didn't deserve this.

"Unless you can come up with another plan, I don't see what else we can do." Dorian stood. "I'm going to see if I can help Junior." He rose and walked away.

"He's right," Randall said, and followed him.

April sighed. How could she make them see that this was a terrible idea? She walked downstairs to where Michael said he'd be. She was keen to learn more about the gate. She'd just have to be careful not to let on that it was the same one.

She found the false wall in front of the gate open, but Michael was nowhere to be found. The gate shimmered with its own dim light. Curious, April approached it. Now that she was seeing it in its full power, it was obvious that the gate in the library was very damaged.

This filled her with deep sadness. The gate, she was coming to realize, was sentient, conscious in a broader way than her puny human brain could fathom. It called out to her, and she reached inside, wanting to feel the mist pass through her fingers. As she did, she was struck by a sense of deep loneliness—not hers, but the gate's. All the other gates were gone; it was the only one left. She could tell that it knew who she was, and what was going to happen to it...

"What are you doing?"

April pulled away. There was a faint glow to her skin where she'd reached her hand through the veil.

"Nothing," she said. "I was just taking a closer look. I've never seen a gate that was fully operational before." She realized what this revealed. "At least not this close up."

If he noticed her slip, he didn't show it. "It is something, isn't it?" he said.

"It sure is." She paused. "Do you really think that we have a chance in this fight?"

He took a moment to answer. "Would you believe me if I said yes?"

"No."

"Well, then why are you asking for?"

She sighed, staring up at the gate. There had to be another way.

He paused for a moment before speaking again. "Now I'm going to tell you something. When I walked over here, you were practically glowing. The gate spoke to you, didn't it?"

She thought for a moment. "Yes, kind of. It wasn't talking, exactly."

"But it was communicating with you." He nodded, as though he'd suspected this all along. "All gatekeepers experience it, though it takes them a while to become attuned with their gate."

"Their gate?" April asked.

"Yes. It happens only with the gate they're bonded with. I couldn't hear your gate, and you couldn't hear mine. Unless, of course they were one and the same."

Her stomach dropped. "I mean..."

Michael shook his head. "Please, no more lies. Not to me. I know your intentions are good, but..." he trailed off, looking up at the gate sadly. "Is she in bad shape?" he asked.

April thought about the ink rot, about the hissing sound every time the gate was opened. "I wouldn't have known the difference before, but after seeing how she's supposed to be... she's not doing well."

He shook his head and closed his eyes. "Over sixty years and we're still fighting the same battle. Is it worth it?"

She thought for a moment. "I think so."

"You've only been in this for so long," he said, smiling ruefully. "Let's talk again when you're my age." He looked away. "When does it happen? Wait—don't tell me. It's better if I don't know." He looked down at his feet. "Do they get my son? Does Junior get hurt?"

"I honestly don't know." April said. She wondered if the documents Thaddeus had brought held the answer. Then she wondered if any of the information it contained was true at all. Probably the folder was empty, a prop.

Michael nodded. "Don't tell Junior. I don't want him to know."

April nodded, glad she wouldn't have to tell anyone else.

Footsteps echoed down the stairs. When April looked up, Dorian stood behind her.

"I'm going to check on Junior," Michael said, and he walked back up the stairs.

"Where's Randall?" April asked Dorian once Michael's footsteps had faded away.

"He's taking Rex out for a walk behind the distillery."

"Possibly the smartest dog in the world and he still has to pee." April shrugged. She looked up at Dorian. "Do you think this will work?"

"We have to try."

"That doesn't answer my question," April said. "I keep asking everyone, and no one can tell me yes. So why are we doing it?"

Dorian looked away without answering.

April sighed. "I'm going to find Randall."

She started to walk out in the direction that Michael had come from when Dorian called, "Wait."

April turned back, surprised by the strain in his voice. Whatever he was about to say wasn't something that came easily to him.

"What is it?" She said, dreading the answer. What else could have gone wrong?

"What the genie said..."

She waved her hand to silence him. "Don't mention it," she said. "It was stupid. I shouldn't have brought it up. He was just trying to get under my skin."

"No," Dorian said. "I mean, yes, he probably was. What I'm trying to say is, he wasn't... wrong."

All the air seemed to rush out of the room, and everything seemed suddenly silent.

"He wasn't?"

Dorian shook his head. "No."

"Oh," she said when the meaning of his words sunk in, and then because she couldn't think of anything else, she repeated it. "*Oh.*"

April stared at Dorian. What should she say? Dorian was jealous of the genie... did that mean he had feelings for her? She'd found Dorian attractive since the moment she'd met him, but who wouldn't? And he was always there for her, even if he was overbearing to the point of annoyance at times... but wasn't that just because he cared?

Dorian sensed her overload. He grasped her hands, as he sometimes did. Before the gesture had always seemed brotherly, but now she didn't know how to feel about it. "Listen. You don't have to do anything, alright? You don't even have to say anything. I just... couldn't bear you not knowing, in case..." he trailed off. "Well, this might be the last time we have a moment in private."

Despite his insistence that she didn't need to talk, she opened her mouth. Still, no words came out.

"Is everything all right?"

They looked back to see Randall and Rex standing at the bottom of the staircase.

"Yes!" April said, pulling her hands out of Dorian's grasp. He let them slip away. She was glad Randall had shown up—it gave her time to think about what Dorian had said. Or more accurately, not think about it. "We were discussing our options."

"Do we have options?" Randall asked, to April's relief. He'd glanced between her and Dorian, obviously sensing something had happened. Luckily, he didn't bring it up.

Dorian shook his head. "Not really, no."

She looked up at the gate. "There has to be another way." She said. "Funny thing is, we're in the same book—world, I mean. Just in the past."

"Yeah," Randall said. "If only we had a time machine."

April was about to reply sarcastically, but then she stopped. An idea sparking in her brain. "Time machine?"

"What is it?" Randall asked, sensing the change in her mood.

"I have an idea," she said. "How far away is the public library?"

~~~

April put the book down on the table in front of everyone.

"The Time Machine?" Dorian asked skeptically. "H. G. Wells is your great master plan?"

"Not H. G. Wells," April said. "The time machine itself." She talked faster, excited now.

"I still don't follow."

"It's so simple it's funny, actually. We got here by census, right? Theoretically we could get back the same way—by finding a census document from our time and going there—except it doesn't work the other way. We don't have access to censuses from the future, and even if we did, it wouldn't be exact enough."

"Uh huh," Dorian said again, still not impressed.

"So we take the time machine, bring it *here* to our world, and then use it to go forward in time."

Dorian cupped his fingers over his nose. "There are so many holes in this plan. Not least of all is the fact that this"—he picked up the book off the table—"is not a key. Werner had to turn the books into keys, remember?"

"Right," April nodded. "Oswald Werner, a self-taught wizard, was able to turn ordinary books like this one into gate keys. We have *two* trained wizards here—why couldn't they do the same?"

Dorian opened his mouth and closed it again several times before saying, "So you're proposing that we go into the world of *The Time Machine*—again, assuming that Michael and Junior can turn this book into a gate key—bring the heavy, *fictional* machine here, and then travel forward in time to the present, and stop the collectors?"

"That's the gist of it."

"How will the time machine get back to its book?" Dorian asked.

"We could take it," Junior said. "Anyway, we don't have a time lock to return it, since our gate is always open."

Randall rubbed his chin and looked at Michael and Junior. "Could you do it? Turn this book into a key?"

Junior whistled. "Not me. You think you could swing this, Pop?"

The elder Michael thought for a moment. "It'll take some freestyling. I'll look at Grandpa Collins' grimoire. He's the one who transferred the threshold into the brick. I may be able to modify that procedure somehow."

"So, are we doing this?" April said. She looked around at everyone.

Michael smiled. "I'll do my best."

April looked down at her watch. They'd been at the distillery for several hours already. It was now nearly midnight in the library. "We'd better hurry."

Chapter Sixteen

Michael went into a separate room in the house. April got the feeling he didn't want them to see what he was doing. That was fine with her, as long as she was able to get back to the present, save Barty, and stop the collectors.

And punch Thaddeus in his stupid, no good, lying face.

The others waited in the sitting room, working out what they would do if Michael succeeded. *When he succeeds,* April reminded herself. She wasn't the only one who was anxious. The others would periodically glance at the door with furrowed brows, and Junior moved in and out of the room more often than necessary.

April was checking her watch for what was probably the twentieth time when Michael came back from the room. He looked haggard, and there were now bags under his eyes that hadn't been there earlier, but he smiled. "I think I did it."

"Let's test it out," April said. They brought the book down to the cellar and opened it. April had chosen a part of the story where the time traveler had left the machine to explore. because it felt like the most likely moment that they'd be able to get the time machine out.

"Here goes nothing," Michael said, and opened the book. The silvery clouds on the other side began to swirl faster. Flashes of lighting illuminated the mist here and there, and April's hair flew around her face in the light breeze. Finally, the clouds' motion stopped, and they began to slowly fade like lifting fog to reveal a dense jungle landscape. In the middle of a clearing they could see the time machine.

"I'll be a monkey's uncle," Michael said. "It worked."

"Let's go," April said.

They ran over to the device. There was no one around, but it was near twilight. "It's almost dark," April said. "After sunset the morlocks come out."

"Morlocks?" Michael Junior asked.

"Cannibalistic human evolutions from the future. Let's go!"

The time machine was surprisingly light. By working together, they were able to carry it back through the gate. She glanced around anxiously just before stepping back over. Glowing red eyes stared back at her through the leaves at the edge of darkness. She shivered and hurried back through the veil.

Chapter Seventeen

Thaddeus had hoped that Mason wouldn't notice his absence. No such luck. When he re-entered the Werner Room, Mason greeted him with, "Nice of you to join us."

Thaddeus shrugged. "I almost forgot I'd arranged to have a drink with one of the Petersens tonight. I didn't want to sour the agency's relationship with them."

Mason approached him, and for a moment Thaddeus thought he was going to strike him. He was surprised when Mason wrapped him in a bear-hug. "Son, your father would be so proud of the man you've become. You've really embraced your new role within the agency. Come on. We're almost done here."

He ended the hug by clapping Thaddeus on the back. As Thaddeus followed him to the edge of the portal, he wondered at Mason's ability to change his demeanor at a moment's notice to work a situation to his advantage.

He also wondered at Mason's ego. Surely he knew that Alan had been placed with the Petersens. Was he so sure of his influence over Thaddeus that he wasn't worried at all?

The agent who'd set up the detection charm looked up at Mason. "Ready when you are, sir." He held a glass jar filled with various objects, a recipe they'd taken from a witch's grimoire. When it was activated, it made any magic within a certain area glow. It was invaluable for finding hidden items after a raid.

Items that are just going into the hands of the rich and powerful, like the Petersens. Like Mason.

Thaddeus pushed the thought away.

Mason nodded. "Let's get this show on the road. My wife is going to kill me for being home this late as it is."

The agent nodded, breaking the glass jar against one of the tables.

Thaddeus grimaced as the pulse from the jar pass through him. Even after all he'd learned—or maybe even *because* of it—he hated magic more than ever. Knowing it was around him, invisible as an airborne virus, made his skin crawl.

The room filled with luminescence as though they were holding a black light over a crime scene. The brightest light came from the stained-glass window itself. You could read a book by it. The next brightest spots were, of course, the books. The entire room—tables, chairs, shelves, even the floor—glowed faintly. Magic corrupted everything, given enough time. It was seeping into his pores at that very moment, becoming part of him. He shivered.

A voice in the back of his head that sounded annoyingly like Alan's tremble whispered, *the magic is already in you, isn't it?*

He couldn't stop himself from looking down at his skin. He was as dark as any of the other operatives, who looked like shadows against the library's slightly-glowing backdrop.

The voice whispered again. *That doesn't mean anything. It's in your blood. You can't see it through your skin.*

"Hmm," Mason said. "It appears that the threshold is embedded within the wall. You know what that means—demolition time, boys."

The operatives began pulling out the crowbars, hammers, and other tools they'd brought for just such a contingency. They began hammering at the brick around the window, starting with the spot they'd deemed the most likely for the threshold to be: directly above the gate.

As the sound of metal striking stone filled the library, Thaddeus decided that he couldn't hold his silence any longer.

"Sir," he said. "May I speak with you in private?"

"Can't this wait until later?" Mason asked, annoyance in his voice. "We're a little busy right now."

"It's pertinent to the matter at hand, sir."

Mason looked at Silvis. "Supervise the boys, sweetheart."

With one last suspicious look in Thaddeus' direction, Silvis followed orders. No matter what, she always followed orders, no questions asked. Was he like that? Blindly following commands?

"What's on your mind, Thad?" Mason asked after they'd walked several paces away.

Thaddeus breathed in before responding. "I have a matter that's been weighing heavily on me. I'm sure it's nothing, but, I'd be more focused on the task at hand if you could dispel some... *rumors* I've heard."

"Rumors?" Mason's eyes narrowed. "Go on."

"Sir..." Thaddeus paused, searching for the best way to phrase his concern that wouldn't offend. He was certain Mason would dispel his doubts, and he didn't want to damage their relationship. Mason was his superior, after all. "At the Petersen fundraiser, I ran into a man who claims to be a wizard. He said he was working for the Petersens."

"An obvious lie," Mason said. "Another agent hoping to get a rise out of you, perhaps a bit of hazing to welcome you to the acquisition management team. Don't be so gullible, Thad."

"I would have thought something similar, sir, except that I saw him being pulled from the prison in the warehouse the day I was promoted. He looked in bad shape. He also wore an iron collar. It seems like a lot of work for a joke."

Mason paused, then laughed as though it were all a big joke. "Okay, son. You caught me."

"So... it's all true?" Thaddeus asked. There had to be some mistake.

"The Petersens have invested heavily in the agency. It only stands to reason that they would want something in return. We are keen to see our partnership with them continue, so we accommodate their requests when possible."

"So you rented out a *wizard* to them? Why keep the wizards alive in the first place?"

"Why not?"

"The conditions they're kept in are atrocious," Thaddeus said. "Death is preferable."

"Since when are you so worried about the treatment wielders? What's the big deal? I thought you hated them."

Thaddeus struggled to find words. He had hated users of magic. He still did. "I kill when it's necessary," Thaddeus said, "What you're doing is... it's just wrong."

Mason turned to Thaddeus. "I've devoted my life to this mission. Do you see anyone *paying* us for what we do? Of course not. We need to survive, as well. Think of the magic as our payment."

This confirmed one of Thaddeus' fears—Alan had been telling the truth. Mason's expensive cars, his houses, his daughter's fancy private school... They were all gotten by magical means, or at least the money that paid for them was.

Mason must have read the disgust on Thaddeus' face, because he leaned in and said, "I wouldn't act so high and mighty if I were you. Those paychecks you cash every month—where do you think that money comes from? Do you think it just appears out of nowhere because we do the *right thing?*" The darkness in Mason's face disappeared, and he smiled that fake, affable smile. "What do you want—a pay raise? That can be arranged." He paused. "Your father was never so disapproving."

His father had known about this. The man who was always ranting about magic, instilling it in the deepest recesses of Thaddeus' psyche that magic was evil. Why?

"I... I need to supervise the operatives," Thaddeus said, and he pushed away from Mason.

Mason called after him. "You're a good soldier, son. Don't think about it too hard. Do the job, get paid. It's what you're good at."

Thaddeus tried to keep his face passive, but a wave of nausea passed over him.

If Alan had been right about this, was he right about his mother as well?

The clock on the wall chimed once. Thaddeus stared at it, both seeing it and not seeing it. There was something off about its face, something that he couldn't quite put his finger on.

Voices by the gate drew his attention away from the clock. They'd found the brick. He walked over. There, not quite at the pinnacle of the arch, was a stone that glowed ten times brighter than the wall behind it; brighter even than the window itself.

"Wonderful," Mason said.

"Should we take it down, sir?" one of the operatives called.

"Not yet," Mason said. "First we have to retrieve our friends."

Mason opened the census book, and the 1940s Minneapolis street appeared in place of the stained glass. It was so picturesque that it could have been a painting come to life. There was only one problem: the Pagewalker and her associates were nowhere to be seen.

"Well, where are they?" Mason said irritably.

"You left them with no guard," Thaddeus said. "Did you really think they would sit there and wait? This portal encompasses the entirety of the city of Minneapolis, and beyond."

"Why didn't you say so earlier?" Mason said, obviously not eager to take the blame. "What do I keep you around for? You're the portal expert."

Thaddeus had had enough of this. "Why *do* you keep me around, Mason? By your own count, I've failed to secure this portal, I've failed to report a meeting with the enemy, and I even sabotaged a mission to secure leverage on the subject. By all cases I should be stripped of my rank at the very least... instead you promoted me. Why? Is it because you don't want me as an enemy?" He leaned in close to Mason, so that only he could hear what he was about to say next. "Is it true? Was my mother a witch? Was her last free act to make it so you can't touch me?"

Mason's eyes grew hard. He didn't back away from Thaddeus, and for a moment Thaddeus thought that he might slap him. Instead, he returned Thaddeus' words in the same low, dangerous tone.

"Thaddeus, I don't know where you heard such a thing. I have put up with your rash behavior out of respect for your father and nothing more. If you prefer that I treat you with harshness, that can be arranged." He turned back towards the gate.

"Where is the Pagewalker?" he yelled.

Thaddeus moved towards one of the windows that overlooked the parking lot. Could he trust anything that Mason had said? He'd kept the truth from him at least twice.

"She's not here," one of the operatives said. He'd stepped away from Mason. He wasn't used to the usually affable Mason displaying such anger. Thaddeus could see by the unsure glances the operatives gave each other that they had all been taken off guard.

"Do you want us to send a group in to find them?"

Mason cleared his throat, bringing himself back under control. He smiled self-indulgently. "No," he said. "They know the laws of balance as much as we do. They'll be back before it closes. Mark my words."

As Mason and the others settled in to wait, movement in the parking lot below caught his eye. Six dark shapes were making their way towards the entrance of the library. Five humans and a dog.

Thaddeus turned to alert the others, but then he closed his mouth. Why? It wasn't that he wanted to help the Pagewalker, per se. But he wouldn't help Mason anymore. Not until he knew the truth.

And he wanted to see what would happen.

~~~

It was a tight fit, but they all managed to fit on the bench-like seat of the time machine. Since April was the smallest, she had to sit on someone's lap. Randall already held Rex, and she decided it was less awkward to sit on Dorian's lap than one of the Michaels'... though not by much.

Dorian kept moving his hands, trying to find a place to put them. With no room on either side of them, they eventually settled into her lap, folded in on themselves as if in prayer.

April suddenly felt hot, and not from the teardrop necklace. Her stomach did a flip as she remembered what Dorian had told her in the barrel cellar... *Focus,* she told herself. *You have no time for distraction.*

Michael was bent over the control panel. All things considered, it was fairly basic. There was a large lever, and next to it a series of rolling numbers that reminded her of a slot machine. A knob increased or decreased the numbers, depending on which way you turned it. "Seems easy enough," he said. "We just have to set this to the correct date and time, and then pull the lever."

"Should we set it for earlier in the day before they show up?" Randall asked. "Then we might be able to keep all of this from happening in the first place."

Dorian shook his head. "We can't. If we stop it all from happening in the first place, then we never go back to stop it from happening, which means it still happens. This creates a—"

"Grandfather paradox," April and Randall supplied in unison.

"What if we don't stop ourselves from going back—we'll just hide out in the shadows? Set a trap or something?" Randall asked.

Dorian shook his head. "There's too much that could go wrong with that. I just hope that this thing with the time machine actually works."

April nodded. "Let's do this as straightforward as possible." She lifted her wrist to indicate Mae's watch. "I know what time it is in the library. We'll go back to that moment and surprise them."

"Surprise I am all for," Dorian said. "What I need to know is what the plan is for beating them. They're going to have more men than us, and weapons."

"Oh," Michael said, grinning a smile that didn't quite reach his eyes. "You leave that to us. You just take care of the gate."

There was a bitter, sad note in his voice that made April think he was out for vengeance. Vengeance for all the gates and keepers that had fallen before him, and vengeance for something that hadn't even happened yet. Vengeance for his son.

He looked at April. "You got that piece of paper, gatekeeper?"

She clutched the note in her hand. On it she'd written, *I retract the invitation of Thaddeus Broker, William Mason, and all their associates. They are no longer welcome in the library.*

Michael glanced at the paper doubtfully. "Are you sure that will work?"

"It did before."

"Right. You just hold onto it good and tight, now."

"Okay," April said. She set the rolling numbers to the correct date and time, then placed her hand on the lever. "Here we go."

I hope this works, she thought, and pushed the lever forward. For a moment, nothing happened. Then the cellar around them began to blur at the edges. They were still in the distillery's cellar. Except for brief flashes of light, they were mostly surrounded by darkness.

Dorian leaned over and whispered in her ear. "We should have checked to see if this cellar still exists in our time," he whispered nervously.

He was right. What if the cellar had been filled in? What would happen to them? Randall's wide eyes showed that he was thinking something similar.

Finally, the whirring of the machine's gears slowed.

"Hold on," April said, and she pulled out her phone and turned on the flashlight. The room was flooded with retina-piercing blue light. She shone the light around the room.

The cellar was still there, though it was only from the half-barrel shape that she recognized it as such. The only evidence of the distillery was a stack of mostly-broken wooden barrels in one corner. The rest of the space had been taken over by years of detritus, unremarkable boxes of all shapes and sizes, a pallet of metal folding chairs, and some tables pushed to the side.

April shone her light at the back of the cellar and immediately wished she hadn't. The back wall was caved in. The spot where the gate had been was no more than a pile of rubble.

An immediate and undeniable sadness flowed over her. She didn't know why she was so shocked by the scene. She'd known the gate wouldn't be there.

The edge of the beam of light illuminated Michael's features in gray-blue light. He looked like a ghost. April could tell that he, too, was feeling the immense sadness.

"Pop," Junior said, "The gate—"

"We must have moved it," he said, shooting a knowing glance at April. "Yeah? Let's go." He sounded eager to leave. April was, too. The place had the somber air of a graveyard.

As they climbed the stairs, deep bass pulsed through the floorboards above their heads. It grew louder the higher they went.

"What is that godawful sound?" Junior said with a look of disgust on his face. "Is someone summoning a demon?"

Randall shook his head. He had to speak loudly to make himself heard over the music. "They turned the distillery into a dance club."

"A what?"

"Like a dance hall," Dorian explained. No one noticed when they emerged through the basement door. Hopefully no one would make their way into the basement for a spare table or set of chairs and find the time machine inexplicably parked there.

If someone unwittingly messed with it and went forward or backward in time, it would be nearly impossible to get it back. Her brain hurt trying to think of the possible consequences.

But she didn't have time to think about that. She had to focus on the problem at hand.

Luckily the library was only a few blocks away. April had dressed for the humid July day in 1940, not a frigid November night. She leaned against Dorian for warmth as they walked down the street. He moved away from her at first, but once he noticed the way her teeth chattered he wrapped his arm around her and squeezed her shoulder comfortingly. The contact sent tingles down her spine.

Focus, she told herself. *You can think about what Dorian said later... if there is a later.*

They reached the parking lot of the library. A purplish glow with green undertones was visible through the Werner Room windows.

"That can't be good," April said.

Michael squinted up at the light. "They've cast a magic detection spell."

"They're looking for the threshold," Dorian said.

"Do you think they've got it?" April asked, her pulse quickening. Were they too late? They were in the real world now, they didn't have the extra cushion of time to plan before acting.

"Most likely."

"Then why are they still there?"

"They're waiting for us," Randall said.

"That's something that's on our side—they can't remove the threshold until they've got us back. Probably gives us a little time."

"Then let's not waste it. Michaels," she said to the wizards. "Are you ready?" They nodded.

"Remember the plan. You guys cause your distraction, and I'll get back to the gate and retract the collectors' invitation." She held the small wad of paper in her palm.

"Dorian and I will cover you," Randall said.

She unlocked the front door as quietly as possible. Every step seemed to creak. Even their breath seemed as loud as a freight train.

They crept up the stairs, pausing to peek around at the turn of each landing, checking for guards. The first and second floors were clear, but Junior raised his hand at the landing below the third floor, signaling for them to stop.

"Two guards are up at the top," he said.

The Michaels whispered to each other for a few seconds, and then nodded.

"We need to make a sound," Michael whispered. "Not loud enough that they yell for help, but we need them to come down the stairs."

"I have an idea," Randall said. He lifted his foot, holding it above one of the creaky stairs. Randall would know better than anyone which stairs made noise. "Ready?"

"Hold on." They pulled out their wands and waved them around their heads with a flourish. As they did, they became darker, as though they were made of shadow. They pressed themselves into the corners at either side of the landing. They were nearly indistinguishable from the shadows of the already-dark stairwell.

"Go ahead."

Randall stepped on the stair. It creaked. Even though they had done it on purpose, April's heart jumped in her chest at the noise.

They held their breath and listened.

"What was that?" One of the guards said.

"Don't be so jumpy, rookie. It's just the foundation settling," the other collector replied, though he didn't sound sure.

Pause. "You're probably right."

Randall lifted his foot and stepped on the stair again.

"I'm going to take a look," the rookie said. His companion didn't argue with him this time. "Should I radio Silvis?"

Uh oh. They needed to take these guards out without alerting anyone in the Werner Room. The element of surprise was the only edge they had, aside from Michael and Junior's magic.

"Only if you want your ass chewed out for wasting her time."

Heavy footsteps banged above their heads. They continued down the stairs and onto the landing where Michael and Junior were disguised as shadows.

A young man dressed in black fatigues appeared at the top of the stairwell. He held a rifle in front of his chest with both hands. He looked around the corner of the stairwell. He made eye contact with April. Surprise appeared in his eyes. Before he could do anything, a shadowy hand shot out of the corner and threw a handful of pink sleep sand in the man's face.

The man's look of surprise shifted to one of confusion, then his eyes rolled up and his mouth fell open. He collapsed downward towards them.

"Catch him!" April whispered. She, Dorian, and Randall caught the man, preventing him from breaking his neck, but making a lot of noise in the process.

"Bill?"

More footsteps rang out as the second guard hurried down the stairs, drawn by the commotion. He didn't even make it down to the landing before a puff of pink appeared in front of his face. He collapsed, the shadows moving forward to catch his fall.

They laid them down gently. They crept up the final half flight of stairs, the Michaels still disguised as shadows.

They paused below the landing, peering over the railing and into the open double doors of the Werner Room. Everyone stood facing the gate, which was opened to the 1940 Minneapolis street that they'd been left in earlier. The man who'd introduced himself as Thaddeus' boss—Mason—was going on about how they weren't there on the other side.

April met Michael's shadowy eyes. He nodded, and she nodded back.

"Go," she whispered, and suddenly everyone was moving towards the Werner Room. The Michaels moved from shadow to shadow.

Shocked, none of the collectors reacted right away.

Mason's back was turned away from them, but Thaddeus's eyes met hers the second they entered the room. *Crap.* She knew she should be moving, but she felt like a deer caught in headlights. They stood like that for several seconds. Why wasn't he pointing her out? He looked almost... bored. As though reading her thoughts, he raised an eyebrow and shrugged.

He's not going to say anything, she thought. She didn't know what that meant, but she doubted he was about to help her.

She decided to discern Thaddeus' mood swings later. Right now, she only had to get the piece of paper in her hand into the gate.

"There they are!"

Her head swiveled towards the source of the voice. An operative near the gate was pointing at them.

"Where?" Mason began looking around, first only through the gate—the logical place where they'd be spotted—but as more and more of the men turned towards the double doors, he turned.

"Oh," he said when he saw them. "How did you get on this side? Someone's been naughty!"

He began to advance on April, but before he could take more than a couple steps, Michael yelled, "NOW, Junior!"

Mason and the operatives began covering their eyes, with their hands and wincing in pain. Their shouts filled the room.

"It's so bright—"

"I can't see!"

"My eyes!"

Others just screamed wordlessly.

The Michaels were again fully visible, as though casting the second spell had negated the first, or maybe they'd decided blending into the shadows was unnecessary, since the operatives so obviously couldn't see. April turned to Michael.

"What's happened to them?" April asked.

Michael grinned. "All they can see is white-hot light. It'll keep them occupied for a few minutes, but that's no reason to dawdle. Go!"

April made her way towards the gate and tossed the piece of paper in. It passed through the veil with a hiss.

She waited for the collectors to be expelled, wondering how it would work now that they couldn't see. Last time it had looked like an outside force was pushing them away.

But nothing happened.

"What are you waiting for?" Dorian yelled at her. "Throw it in!"

"I did," she said back to him. "It didn't work!"

Mason hobbled towards them, gripping the edges of the tables and chairs that he passed by. He obviously couldn't see, but he was handling it better than the others. "Here's the thing," he said in their general direction. "Protection spells like this one are only good from one side, especially weak ones created by amateurs like your friend Mr. Nagles. Once we were in, we dismantled it with ease. Last time we didn't bother. We never expected you to betray Thaddeus. This time we knew better."

He felt around at the opening of his suitcoat, reached inside, and pulled out a tapered stick about half the length of his forearm. It was a wand just like the Michaels'.

"Oh, how does it go again?" he said, tapping the wand against his temple. "Eradico? Eradicato? That one sounds right." He waved the wand around his head. "*Eradicato.*"

Though he still blinked like he'd gotten shampoo in his eyes, his eyes focused on her. He could see again. The same seemed to be happening for the rest of the collectors.

"Jeez," he said, obviously irked by his counter-spell's lack of efficacy. he turned to Michael. "You're a wielder, right? What is it that I'm doing wrong? Did I emphasize the wrong syllable? What?"

Michael spat at Mason's feet. "You did not earn that wand. It can sense you wield it with malice and greed. It will never fully bow to you."

"Hmm," Mason said. "That's a dying shame."

By this time most of the collectors had risen to their feet and were pointing their guns at April and the others, though their eyes were red and watery.

Mason stepped towards April. "You should have accepted my job offer. The fact that you're here is a testament to your will and intellect. What you might have become with us to guide you."

Off to her right, April could see Junior raising his wand. He began to speak, but before he could get out even the first syllable, Mason had raised his hand, and with a flick, Junior had frozen in place.

"How's that for bending magic to my will?" Mason said with a grin.

Michael let out a pained shriek. He charged Mason like a madman, his wand raised.

With a flick of Mason's wrist, he too, was frozen, motionless, flesh made statue.

Mason walked towards the inert forms, pulling their wands from their hands. They came free with sick tearing sounds, as though he'd pulled away some skin along with the wands.

Mason pocketed his bounty. "Now, where were we?"

~~~

Thaddeus couldn't believe what he was seeing. He'd known Mason had used magic to accumulate his wealth and power, but this... this was an abomination. It went against everything the agency stood for. Mason now wielded more power than any wizard or witch Thaddeus had worked against.

"What are you doing, Mason? Wielding magic?"

Mason shook his head as though shooing away a mosquito that had been buzzing in his ear. "Would you *stop* with your incessant whining?" He said. "So what if I'm using magic? I deserve it. *We* deserve it. Do you think these inconsequential *fools* deserve it? No! Look at them, scared for their lives."

"This is wrong, Mason," Thaddeus said.

"Says the half-witch operative! That's right—everything Alan told you was true." He sighed. "Ah, that feels good to get off my chest. And you know what's worse? Your father *knew*. He knew who she was. She seduced him with her magic, but he didn't care."

"No," Thaddeus said. "My father hated magic."

"Yes, he did. That much is true. I don't know how he reconciled his love for you with his hatred for what flows through your veins, but he did. That's why he never went after that she-witch in jail. He knew to do so would endanger your life. I didn't find out until the spell she put upon you was well in place. It was powerful stuff. I had teams working on removing it—your father never knew—but no luck."

"I will not stand for this," Thaddeus said. He couldn't process the things that Mason was saying at that moment. All he knew was that he had to stop him.

Mason raised an eyebrow. "Oh? What exactly are you going to do?"

Thaddeus gritted his teeth. Mason was right. There was nothing he could do to stop him, not when he had three wands in his hand and had two dozen agents at his command.

"That's what I thought. Fall in line. Let the true leaders lead. It's what you're best at."

Thaddeus caught the Pagewalker looking at him. She was a magic-wielder of sorts, true, but her sins paled in comparison with Mason's. The whole agency was corrupt. Had anything Thaddeus ever believed been true?

Mason turned back to the gate. "Now that our friends have returned from their trip back in time," Mason said, "Let's retrieve that threshold."

Two of the operatives, their light-scorched eyes still streaming, began to pry the brick in question loose from the wall. Once it was loose, it would be added to the agency's hoard of magic. With no other recourse available to him, Thaddeus had no choice but to watch it happen.

One side of the brick loosened first. The operatives grunted as they put pressure on the crowbar, and the brick came free with the crunch and crack of the wall behind it. As they pulled it out, he noticed the brass plaque attached to the side that had faced into the wall. He moved closer to read it: *Collins Distillery & Spirits founded 18—*. The final two digits had been chipped away so the exact year wasn't legible.

He squinted at the plaque. There was something familiar about the numbers; he couldn't place his finger on it...

The operative who'd removed the threshold gently blew off the excess brick dust, then held it out to Mason as though presenting a sacrificial object to a vengeful deity.

The poor sap had no idea that Mason would most likely kill him and every operative in the room after the job was done. At the very least they'd be locked up. They'd all seen Mason admit to using magic for his own personal gain—that wasn't something Mason could afford to get out to the lower-ranking agents.

Mason took the threshold triumphantly, but his expression soon shifted to one of dismay. "If this is the threshold," he said, "Then why is the portal still open?"

It was true; the gate remained open still, unchanged.

"It's chipped," Mason said, rubbing his fingers over the missing digits. "You morons!" he barked at the operatives. "It's broken! Where are the missing pieces?"

The operatives scrambled to action, combing through the bits of broken brick at the base of the window and peering into the hole above it where the threshold had been. Thaddeus could tell that each one was worried they might be the next fall under Mason's magical ire.

The grandfather clock in the corner began to chime. One ring, then two. Everyone was so concerned with the missing piece that they didn't even register the sound—everyone except Thaddeus.

He started to think of the mismatched numbers on the clock's face. Had he just imagined it? The distillery had opened in 1859. They'd learned that in the hours after April had revealed what the threshold was. The gate opened each night at nine and closed again in the morning at five. Such a coincidence was possible, though not likely. Especially when magic was involved.

No one noticed when Thaddeus strode over to the grandfather clock and opened its face. The nine and the five *were* different. Slightly too large, and they protruded from the clock's face a bit further than the other numerals. A glowing pinprick as bright as the threshold itself lit was visible on the edge of the five. He reached out, pausing a moment, loathe to touch such potent magic directly. Then he brushed it ever-so-gingerly with only his fingernail, and scratched. As he removed the paint covering the letters, the glow hidden behind the paint spread. He continued to scratch, still unnoticed within the chaos of the room, like he was using a lottery ticket, until the bright luminescence of the nine and the five was only marred by the thinnest flecks of paint here and there.

Not caring if anyone saw him, he took out the knife strapped to his belt, and slid it carefully beneath the numbers. A couple minutes later, he held them in the palm of his hand. Each was about an inch long. He expected them to burn his skin because they shone so brightly, but they were cool to the touch.

"Where are they!" Mason shrieked, and Thaddeus began to laugh.

He just couldn't believe it, how Oswald Werner had tricked them. Obscuring the magic with a thin coat of paint? He hadn't even told the Jackson woman! He gripped them in his palm.

He was laughing so hard now that the others started to turn towards him, confused. First the Pagewalker, then her friends, then some of the operatives, then finally, at the last, Mason.

This made Thaddeus laugh harder. He was laughing so hard that he was crying, and not just from the wizard's curse.

Mason crossed his arms like a disapproving father. "What's so funny? Care to share with the class?"

"It was right in front of us this whole time," Thaddeus said. "The gate opens at nine and closes at five. Did anyone ever stop to ask *why?* That's not normal. It wouldn't just happen. Someone had to *make it* that way. Someone had to *choose* it." He wiped at the corners of his eyes.

Everyone looked at it him like he was crazy.

"It's the *clock,*" he said, as though explaining a joke.

"You've gone mad," Mason said.

"Have I?" Thaddeus opened his hand, revealing the glowing numerals nestled in his palm.

Mason stepped towards Thaddeus. He grinned, but it didn't quite reach his eyes. "Looks like I spoke too soon. Can you blame an old man? Good work, son. Your skills of deduction are astounding." He held his hand out towards him. "I'll take those."

Thaddeus backed away. "No."

"Thaddeus," Mason said placatingly. "It's me, Mason. Your mentor, your friend. You can trust me."

Thaddeus said nothing.

Mason gestured to the wand. "Is it because of this thing? I checked it out this morning in preparation for this mission. You can ask Whitney and Jane. I only use magic when it's necessary. You know that."

Thaddeus shook his head. "That's not going to work on me this time, Mason. I've seen the truth."

"Pity." The smile fell away from Mason's face, and his eyes grew cold. "Well, it seems we're at an impasse, doesn't it? I have this part of the threshold, you have that part."

The Pagewalker spoke up. "The numbers are more powerful," she said. "See how much brighter they are?"

Thaddeus looked down at the numbers in his hand. It was true, they *were* brighter than the brick Mason held, though they hadn't started out that way. Their brightness had been equal when he first pulled them from the clock. Yet it was undeniable. Even now the numerals were getting brighter, just as the stone in Mason's hand was becoming dull, just another brick.

"The magic is shifting," Dorian, the character, said.

"The gate is doing it," the Pagewalker said. The look in her eyes was faraway, as though she were listening to a distant voice and had to concentrate to make out what it was saying.

She turned to Thaddeus. "She trusts you."

Who trusted him? The gate?

"I'm not on your side." Thaddeus took a step away from her. "I just don't want *him* to have them."

"This is trying my patience," Mason said angrily. He cast the now quite-dull brick away. It clattered on the floor under one of the desks. "Agent Silvis—secure the threshold. Do not hurt Agent Broker—the agency will discipline him later."

Silvis stepped away from the Pagewalker, her mouth curved in a sharp, feline smile. The other agents—at least the ones that weren't guarding the Pagewalker and her friends—followed her, their guns trained on Thaddeus.

He backed away from the operatives, but it was no use: there were too many of them. They'd easily be able to hold him down and pry the threshold from his hands...

The nearest operative stepped forward and grabbed the wrist of the hand that was holding the numbers, but before he could pry it open Thaddeus reared back and struck him in the face with his free hand.

The man screamed, and one of the other operatives aimed their gun at him and pulled the trigger.

Thaddeus saw the gun and heard the blast, but there was no time for him to dodge or move away from the bullet's path. He could tell that it would strike him in the shoulder. Well, it wouldn't be the first time that he'd been shot. He closed his eyes and braced for the impact, determined to keep hold of the numbers no matter what.

The impact never came.

Instead, Mason screamed. Thaddeus looked up at him as a splotch of bright red appeared on his shoulder.

Thaddeus looked around for whoever had shot him, but all the operatives were facing Thaddeus, and none of the Pagewalker's people had guns. The operative who had shot at Thaddeus kept glancing from the gun to Thaddeus to Mason, sweat breaking out on his forehead.

Alan had said that the last thing his mother had ever done as a free woman was put a charm on Thaddeus protecting him from the agency. The agency, or Mason? Or was it any ranking official in the agency? Why had Mason been hurt and not the man who pulled the trigger?

There was only a split second for Thaddeus to ponder these things.

"*I said not to hurt him!*" Mason shrieked, clutching at his shoulder. Two operatives rushed over to tend to him, but he pushed them off. "Get away from me. Put down your guns, all of you!" His voice was panicked, and the agents all looked at him, not quite believing what he was telling them to do. "Now! Any agent holding a gun in five seconds will be court-marshalled!"

This time, they listened. The library was filled with the sound of metal clanking against the hardwood.

Mason continued to shout. "Do I have to do all the heavy thinking around here? *We outnumber them!* Hold him down and take the threshold!"

~~~

April couldn't believe what she'd seen. She'd watched the bullet rocket towards Thaddeus' shoulder, had even braced sympathetically for its impact—but Mason had taken the blow instead.

She didn't have enough facts to explain this, and the sweet, faint almost-voice she'd heard a few minutes earlier remained silent on the matter. All she knew was that it was better for Thaddeus to have the threshold than Mason.

And then, even more absurd, Mason had ordered all his men to put down their guns—and they did. Including the three who were guarding them.

Everything slowed down, as though someone had reduced the playback speed of a television. All three of the guards were looking away from them. They were preoccupied with following Mason's orders. That wouldn't last long.

Without thinking, April bent down and reached for the gun the guard in front of her had just put down on the floor. She could see his foot moving to kick it out of her reach—but not fast enough.

Her hands closed around it. As she stood, she brought the butt of the gun straight up and struck the guard in the nose. Before his hands had even come up to clutch his face, she stepped to the left and knocked the guard that stood in front of Randall in the temple. He crumpled to the ground. She stepped back to the right. The remaining guard wore a helmet, so she pushed her palm into his diaphragm, knocking the wind out of him. He bent over, and fell to his knees, his mouth visible through his visor opening and closing like a fish as he struggled to breathe in.

Everything returned to normal speed. She stared at the gun in her hand for a moment. When she looked up, both Dorian and Randall were staring at her.

"What just happened?" Randall asked.

"Pagewalker sense," Dorian said.

April nodded, then brought the gun against the temple of the guard with the broken nose. He fell to the ground.

She handed the gun to Randall. "You're the only one who knows how to use this."

Her hands shook as he pulled it away. "I don't know about that. You seem like you're doing okay." He examined the gun and shook his head. "It has a fingerprint scanner on the trigger. It's useless." He pushed it and the other guns the three guards had dropped under a nearby shelf.

She ignored his concerned tone. "We have to help Thaddeus."

Neither Dorian or Randall argued with her.

Since Mason told the operatives to drop their guns, they were in less danger of being shot... but they were still outnumbered four to one.

Dorian picked up a step stool and began swinging it at any collector who approached him. Randall and a snarling Rex ran after a group that were approaching Thaddeus. April saw a female collector heading for Thaddeus, and she reached out with her foot and tripped her. She tumbled to the floor.

"Thaddeus!" April yelled. "Over here!"

Whether Thaddeus heard her or not, or if he would heed her call either way, April didn't know. Three collectors had ahold of him. One held his free arm pinned to his side, the other two were reaching for the numbers, which he held in his hand high above his head like a beacon. He kneed one of them in the crotch, and the man bent down into the fetal position.

Still, Thaddeus wouldn't be able to hold out much longer.

"It's no use..." Thaddeus said. Another collector bear hugged him from behind, and he struggled to remain standing.

He glanced over at her for a second.

Then he brought that hand down to his mouth. When he brought it away, it was empty. His Adam's apple bobbed up and down. He grimaced like he'd swallowed a gigantic horse pill.

He'd eaten the threshold.

His expression grew pained. He allowed the collectors to grab his hand and pry it open.

"It's not here!" one of them said.

"What do you mean it's not there?" Mason yelled. "He must have hidden it! Find it! *Do not* harm him!"

How could the other collectors have not seen what he'd done? April watched him. He'd swallowed it. That hadn't been a ploy, and yet...

The operatives searched the floor by his feet and tore into his clothing but found nothing. Mason kept screaming for the collectors to find it.

April kept expecting Thaddeus to protest, but he only stared ahead, glassy eyed, allowing himself to be moved and positioned like a doll. His face was ghostly pale.

~~~

Thaddeus didn't feel well. He'd known, somehow, as he swallowed the threshold that it was the only way to stop Mason from getting it. He hadn't thought beyond that.

At first, he'd felt only the vague discomfort of having swallowed something that wasn't meant to be ingested. He'd gotten past his gag reflex by telling himself it was the same thing as swallowing a couple pills—extra-large, sharp-edged horse pills to be sure, but still only pills. They'd scratched going down, leaving the slightly-electric taste of metal in his mouth. His belly immediately felt queasy.

But the queasiness soon erupted into a vibrating energy. Heat. But no, that wasn't quite right. It was more than that, like electricity and fire together.

This heat moved its way out from his stomach, down his legs and into his toes, up his arms and out into his fingertips, and up to the base of his spine. As it reached his face, he felt like his eyes had been opened—both figuratively and literally. The world around him seemed brighter, and he noticed more, like the quick pulse in the jugular of the nearest agent, and the click of the mechanism inside the grandfather clock behind him.

But there was more than just the physical enhancement. He was suddenly, in one blinding, white-hot moment, aware of all the pain he had caused. Him, and the agency. The families that had been torn apart, the magic that had been hoarded. The images flooded his brain, too many to take in in more than just a general flash: the scared eyes of a child as he hides while his parents are being taken away in chains, at first to be hanged, but then, later, with the addition of terrible and immense greed, to be locked away and used like chattel. The kindly healer who used her magical gifts to heal the inhabitants of her village forced to spend the rest of her days in a cage.

These, he learned, were the *small* things. He saw great monoliths, the things they knew as *gates* or *portals,* being dismantled and taken down, hidden away if only because men like Mason hadn't yet learned how to bend them to their will. This made the world sick, uneven, *unbalanced,* even if the true consequences of it hadn't yet formed (as everything with the monoliths happens slowly when seen through human eyes), and those symptoms which had occurred were un-noticeable.

How could he have known that the gates were sentient? He was sharing his head with one right at that very moment. It was both compassionate and cruel, invested and uncaring.

To the monolith's credit, it showed him the good as well as the bad. He learned that some wizards and witches (who were not so very different from men like Mason) were evil and power hungry and cruel, and it was in response to these magic-wielders that the agency was formed. At first it was only a small collection of well-intentioned men and women, but that as it grew in power, it twisted and became corrupted.

He was shown, instantly, that neither the agency (at least in its earlier form) nor the wielders were *wrong,* necessarily—it was more correct to say that they were both right and both wrong, just in different ways about different things.

All of this he saw in a fraction of an instant that lasted a thousand years.

Why do you show me this? He asked the monolith in his head.

Because the wrongs must be made right, a voice answered.

When his hand lifted, it wasn't him lifting it—at least he didn't think it was; the lines between him and the monolith had become so... muddled. He watched as his palm flattened and each of the operatives went flying across the room.

~~~

April watched in a mixture of awe and horror at the scene taking place in front of her. A few seconds after Thaddeus swallowed the numbers, his entire body began to glow as bright as the threshold had been itself.

He raised his hand and flattened it, and every operative within ten feet of him was thrown into the air. They crashed into the shelves, sending books flying off the shelves.

She watched as his head turned towards her, and his eyes glowed even brighter than the rest of him. He looked at her for a few seconds, then turned away. He faced Mason.

"Restrain him!" Mason yelled, his eyes wide. He took a step backwards and kept moving in that direction until he collided with a chair, being forced to sit in it. It was almost comical.

Thaddeus continued to walk towards Mason. As evil as he was, April couldn't help feeling sorry for the man.

"Thad," Mason said. "We can fix this. What do you want? A million dollars? A tropical island somewhere with your name on it? Just tell me what it is, and it's yours."

Thaddeus remained inert. It was... *creepy,* the way his face revealed no emotions at all. He moved towards Mason until he was a few feet in front of him. He stopped moving.

Mason took this as a good sign. "Whoah, sport," he said with a nervous chuckle. "You scared me there for a second. But of course, you wouldn't do anything to your old pal Mason, right? You know that I'm just doing my job, right? Thad?"

Thaddeus' mouth opened, but the voice that came out wasn't his. "I am not Thaddeus."

The voice was both human and not. If April had to pick a gender, she would have said it was a woman's voice. It was also familiar, though she'd never heard it so clearly before.

"It's the gate," she whispered.

"What?" Randall said. Dorian, who had come over to stand next to them once the collectors had stopped paying attention to him, also looked at her, confused.

"It's the gate. He's the gate. It's in him."

"How is that possible?"

"I don't know."

Mason made a choking sound. He croaked out, "What do you want? I'll give you anything."

Thaddeus' head cocked to the side. "You have nothing I want," the gate said, and Mason blanched. "and if you did, you are the type of man who breaks promises like they are made of thread."

"Anything," Mason sobbed. "I have a daughter."

"Every person you have ever hurt had loved ones. What mercy did you show them?"

Mason lowered his head as if to sob, but then thought better of it. He rose from the chair. He knocked it over in the process, and tripped on it, stumbling to the ground.

To April's surprise, the gate allowed him to run for the stairwell. She thought he was going to escape, but a foot away from the double doors he froze mid-stride, completely motionless. He began to glow red, brighter and brighter, his face contorting into a look of pain. Then he exploded into a cloud of dust that disappeared before it fell onto the carpet, leaving only his clothes behind.

The gate that was Thaddeus stood, staring at the spot where Mason had once been. The gate's sorrow and rage radiated from it. April felt every emotion as if it were her own. Despite the gate's anger, it would have preferred to show Mason mercy—but his death was necessary.

Thaddeus turned to face the group of collectors, some had taken their guns from the ground and pointed them at Thaddeus.

One collector let a round fly. The bullet stopped inches in front of Thaddeus' face. He stared at it, then cocked his head. It glowed, much like Mason had, and then burst into dust. With another cock of his head, the barrel of every gun in the room twisted in on itself. Several of the collectors screamed and dropped their guns, but a few just stared at the ruined firearms in disbelief.

Thaddeus/the gate considered the operatives for a moment. Finally, the gate spoke once more, exhaustion coloring her voice, "Go. If any of you ever rejoin the agency, you will meet the same fate as your leader. Do you doubt that I possess the power?"

Most of the collectors were frozen in place, their eyes wide, but a few managed to shake their heads.

"Good. Go."

Most of the collectors ran for the stairwell, but the blond woman—Silvis—remained still. She'd been the agent closest to Mason when he'd exploded, and she bent down to examine his clothing for a few moments before standing again. She watched Thaddeus calculatedly, then she turned towards April.

It was the first time April had seen her without a demented smile on her face. This time her features were twisted into a mask of fury. Her expression told April that this wasn't over. Not by a long shot.

They held eye contact for a few more seconds, and then Agent Silvis followed the rest of the collectors down the stairwell.

Once they were all gone, Thaddeus/the gate approached them. Randall and Dorian tensed up, and Rex whimpered and hid behind Randall's legs. But April wasn't afraid.

Thaddeus/the gate stopped a few feet away. "They will send others," the gate said, "But they won't be here for a long while. You have time."

"Time for what?" April said.

"To prepare." He turned away from them. "I must go now. Goodbye."

He (she?) began to walk away. Panic rose in April's chest. Where was he going?

"Wait!" she called, and he turned back. "What if we need you again?"

"That is... unwise. I am not meant to be in this form. Already it wearies me. All these... *thoughts.*" He paused. "Your bodies aren't designed to take it. Your friend's mind is already beginning to crack."

"He's not our friend," Dorian said.

"Are you sure?" The gate cocked Thaddeus' head to the side. "Maybe I have chosen the wrong word. He did just help you."

"For his own reasons."

"He, too, is a victim in this. And a perpetrator. But isn't everyone?"

He approached Michael and Junior, touching each in turned. He caressed the elder wizard's cheek with something akin to tenderness; familiarity. Then he stood.

"They will wake soon. They cannot see this."

April nodded. Thaddeus walked over to the clock and touched its face. The glow that permeated his body slowly drained out of him, returning to the grandfather clock, this time permeating it in its entirety. The gate reappeared, showing the 1940 Minneapolis street scene. April hadn't even noticed the gate closing in the first place.

Once all the color had drained out of him, Thaddeus swayed for a few seconds, then toppled to the ground.

April ran over to him. "Are you okay?" she said. Randall and Dorian came to stand next to her, moving more reluctantly.

Thaddeus didn't move right away, and for a few seconds she thought that he was dead. But then he blinked, and his eyes opened. Her first reaction was one of relief, but then she saw the way his eyes failed to focus on her. They appeared to be looking *through* her.

"I saw... I saw I saw I saw..."

"What did you see?" Randall said. If he had had any qualms about who he was talking to, his voice didn't show it.

"Everything," Thaddeus said, and a single tear rolled down his cheek. "The lights in the sky and the fire down below and their screams... oh, all the screams..."

He kept babbling incoherently.

"What's wrong with him?" April asked, though she already knew.

"He shared his mind with the gate," Dorian said. "It was too much for him."

"How long will it last?" she said.

Dorian just shook his head.

"But what about Barty?" she grabbed Thaddeus' shoulders, forcing him to look at her. "Thaddeus!" She spoke clearly, staring straight into his eyes. He turned towards the sound of her voice. "Where did they take Barty? How do we get him back?"

"Impossible, impossible... like a camel passing through the eye of a needle or getting to the center of a star without burning up first. So many doors, so many keys."

She shook him. "That can't be it!" she said. "We can't just let them kill him."

"No, not kill," Thaddeus said, his forehead wrinkling with effort. "Keep. They will keep him."

He looked up at her, and his gaze became more serious, and for a second she thought that he was coming back to, regaining a little bit of his former sanity. "I'm sorry. It had to be this way." he said. Then his vision clouded again. "So many doors, so many keys..."

Groaning from the other side of the room drew their attention. The Michaels were waking up. "Stay with him," April said to Randall, and he nodded.

She and Dorian walked over to the Collins. "Are you okay?" she asked.

They were rubbing their heads and grumbling, but they nodded. "Did we win?" Junior asked.

She paused for a moment before nodding.

When Junior walked over to check on Thaddeus, April told Michael about the gate.

Michael looked over at Thaddeus, shaking his head. "The gates are on a higher level than us," he said. "That kind of knowledge and power isn't meant to be held in the human mind. I hate to feel sorry for a collector, but..." he shook his head. "What will you do with him?" he asked.

"I don't know," April said. "He helped us, though. Didn't he? But did he do it because he wanted to help *us,* or because he didn't want to help Mason anymore?"

Michael thought for a moment. "Again, I hate to sound sympathetic to a collector—even a former collector—but it sounds like he was trying to do the right thing, at least in his mind. In the end he chose right."

April nodded. "We'll see what we can do for him."

~~~

April and Dorian walked the Michaels back to the time machine, leaving Randall and Rex to watch Thaddeus. The night club had since gone dark, and none of the people milling outside of it reacted when they kicked in an aging side door. When they walked down the stairs, the time machine was right where they left it. At least something had gone right.

"We'll get her back where she belongs," Michael said, hitting the front of the time machine like it were a faithful old car. "Of course, we aren't bound to the nine-to-five schedule that you all are, so maybe we'll take her for a spin, first." He grinned conspiratorially. "There has to be some perks to this line of work. In fact..." he reached into his pocket and pulled out Mason's wand. "I picked it up while retrieving our wands. You should have it. Something tells me you need it more than us."

April took the wand. It felt strange in her hand, no more than a thick twig. "I don't know how to use this."

Michael shrugged. "You'll figure it out."

They climbed behind the wheel. "Remember," Michael said. "We're just one page away if you need us."

He pushed the lever down, and then the time machine vibrated. Then they were gone.

She and Dorian walked back to the library.

"How are we going to get him back?" she asked.

She didn't need to say his name for Dorian to know she was talking about Barty. He thought for a moment. "I don't want to lie, April," he said. "It won't be easy. Even if Thaddeus is right about them not killing wizards. Hundreds of American otherkin have been taken by the collectors. I haven't heard any stories of any of them coming back."

"But we have one thing that they don't have," April said. "We have inside information. We have Thaddeus."

"Even if his mind recovers enough to be of use to us, we still don't know if he wants to help us," Dorian said. "He tricked us once before. But... you're right. We do have some cause to hope."

April nodded. They walked several blocks in silence. "So, are we not going to talk about what you said?"

Dorian breathed out. "I was hoping we wouldn't."

"Is it true? Do you really feel that way?"

"I—" Dorian stopped talking, his hand forming a claw in the air in front of his face, as though grasping for the right words. "I was annoyed when you started visiting the genie. I told myself it was because I didn't want you distracted. But then I realized it was something more."

April was speechless. Of course, she'd found Dorian attractive—anyone would—but that was overshadowed by fighting the collectors and taking care of the gate. But why had she told Gram that her lover's name was Dorian... and what about that night in Groundsville where, for a split moment, she'd thought Dorian was leaning in to kiss her... and she wouldn't have stopped him.

She opened her mouth to speak—to say what, she still wasn't sure—but Dorian spoke first.

"You don't have to say anything," he said. "This is nothing but an infatuation, I'm sure of it." He took her hands in his own again, just as he had in the barrel cellar. Her stomach flipped. "Soon it will fade to the love of a friend, a brother. It will not impede our work, you have my word." He kissed her hands chastely, then released them.

"Is that what you want?" She said, her voice faltering.

"It's what's best."

They continued back to the library. He was right—it *was* for the best. Even if she had wanted something more, and she wasn't sure that she did, there was so much that could go wrong. What if the relationship went sour? How would it affect the others? Anyway, she needed to be focused on getting Barty back...

Her hands buzzed where his lips had touched them. She wiped at them, as though she could brush away the feeling. But the feeling didn't go away.

Chapter Eighteen

Gram shrieked from the living room.

April jumped out of bed. She'd arrived home only hours before.

April followed the sound, fearing the worst—had the collectors come for them so soon? The gate had promised they had time... April clutched the teardrop pendant. It was cool to the touch.

Not reassured, she hurried out to the living room.

"Gram—are you okay?"

Gram stood by the front door, her hand over her mouth. In the other she clutched a stack of letters and junk mail. She stared down at the topmost letter, which she'd already removed from the envelope.

April's heartrate slowed, but she still wasn't at ease. What could make Gram shriek like that?

"What happened?" April asked. "Are you hurt?"

Gram held up the letter. Her hand shook. April squinted down at the paper and recognized the Senior Star logo. Uh-oh.

"We were selected!" Gram said. "They're going to send us on a ten-day European vacation!" her eyes teared up. "But how? I never mailed the entry form." She looked up at April, realization blooming on her face.

April smiled weakly. "I found your letter and decided to mail it. I didn't say anything because I didn't want to get your hopes up."

"Oh, honey," Gram said. "I can't believe you did that." She came over and hugged April, still clutching the letter in her hand. April patted Gram's back. She should be ecstatic... but how could she go? Who would watch the gate? What would she tell Gram? They still needed to get Barty back. Part of her wished she had never sent in the entry form, but how could she feel that way when it made Gram so happy?

Gram pulled away from her and returned to the letter. "There's a number to call," she said. "We'll talk to their in-house travel agents to schedule our for trip next week."

"Next week?" April squeaked, walking over to look down at the letter. "So soon?"

"I have terminal cancer, April," Gram said. "It's not like I can schedule it for next year."

Of course. An agency that granted wishes to people with terminal diagnoses would want to schedule things as soon as possible to ensure that the recipients would be well enough to enjoy them.

"I don't know if I can take off that much time that soon," April said, trying to plant the seeds so that Gram wouldn't be let down *too* hard when she found out April couldn't go. "Maybe you can ask one of your friends to go with you?"

"Don't be ridiculous," Gram said. "The whole point of this trip is for us to spend time together. If you're not there, then there's no point in me going. Anyway, the library didn't seem to mind that much when you called in for a week straight."

Gram was right about that. As far as the library was concerned, her position was more of a figurehead than anything. This was especially true after Janet was promoted to take care of the items in the vault. They only kept her around to keep the Werner funding for the library. She took care of small tasks, but if she wasn't there the only thing they had to worry about was covering the third-floor reference desk—something she'd discovered that the downstairs L.A.s enjoyed, as it was less busy than the rest of the library.

Gram squinted down at the letter. "Anyway, it says here that one of their partner companies is an employment agency that will provide a temporary replacement if necessary."

Uh oh. If April couldn't say that the reason she couldn't go was the library, what would she tell Gram?

"That's... great, Gram," April said, unable to think of anything else. "I'm excited."

"You don't sound like it."

"I guess I'm still in shock. Honestly, when I sent that letter in I never believed we'd be selected."

"You and me both, hon," Gram said with a smile. She fluttered her fingers excitedly. "I have to call Rita and let her know! She'll flip!"

April watched Gram hurry back to the kitchen to find her cell phone with a sinking feeling in the pit of her stomach. She'd travelled back in time, dealt with the ink rot, and beat the collectors—twice.

But how was she going to get out of this?

~~~

Thanks for reading this ARC of *Wordeater,* book three in the Library Gate Series!

I will send out the link to leave a review as soon as it is available.

Thanks for reading!

You just finished *Wordeater,* the third book in the Library Gate Series. Thanks so much for reading!

If you liked this book, consider leaving an honest four- or five-star review on Amazon because it will help other readers find a book they'll enjoy and will also let me know that you want more books written in the Pagewalker series! It can be as simple as "I liked it!"

Here's an easy to remember link where you can leave a review: **www.hdukeauthor.com/review-wordeater**.

You'll also want to sign up for my reader group, because you'll get free copies of *The Fiction Room (*the short story that the Library Gate Series is based on) and *The First Adventure of Braddy Evers,* the book that April and her friends went into to save Rico in *Spinebreaker,* and more!

You can sign up by visiting this link: **www.hdukeauthor.com/reader-group-wordeater**.

See you in book four!

-H. Duke

More books by H. Duke

Fantasy
Jeremiah Jones Cowboy Sorcerer Series
Jeremiah Jones Cowboy Sorcerer: The Complete First Season
Season One Episode One
Season One Episode Two
Season One Episode Three
Season One Episode Four
Season One Episode Five
Season One Episode Six
Season One Episode Seven
Season One Episode Eight
A Cowboy Sorcerer Christmas (reader group exclusive)
Taming the Wolf (reader group exclusive)
The Pagewalker Series
Pagewalker
Spinebreaker
Wordeater
The First Adventure of Braddy Evers (reader group exclusive)
Horror (written as H. H. Duke)
Things on the Shelf: Three Tales of Christmas Terror
Find an up-to-date list at *http://www.hdukeauthor.com*

About the Author

H. Duke has written over ten works of fiction, including the weird west serial *Jeremiah Jones Cowboy Sorcerer* and the Library Gate series.

These days, she can be seen travelling the United States in her travel trailer with her husband Giru and a shiny black dog named Jupiter. To see an up-to-date list of her works and find out where she'll be writing next, visit *http://www.hdukeauthor.com.*

www.ingramcontent.com/pod-product-compliance
Lightning Source LLC
Chambersburg PA
CBHW052003170626
46808CB00007B/2753